LEILA

LEILA

A Novel

Prayaag Akbar

FABER & FABER

First published in 2018
by Faber & Faber Ltd
Bloomsbury House
74–77 Great Russell Street
London WC1B 3DA

Typeset by Faber & Faber Ltd
Printed in the UK by CPI Group (UK) Ltd, Croydon CRO 4YY

A CIP record for this book
is available from the British Library

ISBN 978–0–571–34131–3

2 4 6 8 10 9 7 5 3 1

For Amma and Abba

THE WALL

My husband thinks we cannot find her. His voice is raw from screaming. 'When will you understand, Shalini? It's been sixteen years.'

'You think I don't know?'

Riz looks at me, bobbles his head but doesn't say anything. In the sinking light his old-man stubble glitters like salt grain. It is he who doesn't understand. I'm almost there.

As we walk from the broad pavement to a small rectangle of grass he pulls out two candles from the satchel. Purity One stretches out across us to the edges of the dusk, either end into the swirling ash. Gritty grey brick. Sixty feet high. Wrapping around the political quarter, sealing off the broad, tree-lined avenues, the colonial bungalows, the Ministries, the old Turkic gardens.

Standing where we are now the wall is shimmering. Broad iridescent streaks, shifting in the way green and brilliant purple dance on the throat of a pigeon. (Pigeons infest this place.) Purity One is believed to have an inscrutable power. People come here to pray and plead. Take my own situation. I should be standing alone, yet here Riz is, by my side, etched sharp against the dusk as anything around us.

Not far from where we are there is a small room abutting the wall. On the roof a white flag flutters, black pyramid, white tip. Hundreds of people shoulder past each other to get to this room. In the great heave all we see is a trapezoid of blue light where the double door extends above the devotees. There is a low cage in the room that everyone surges towards, diving to the ground with half-bleats and cries. Behind the thin wire bars is the holy centre of the wall: middle of the lowest line of bricks, painted ochre-like red. They worship this brick. They call it the first brick of Purity One.

Riz knelt to dig a hole in the earth. His back is badly hunched. Once there was a curving furrow of pebble-like muscles under each shoulder blade from hours every day on the squash court, but now, bent over the ground, he looked as a tortoise does when it retreats into its shell.

I got down beside him, creaky myself. 'These are different candles,' I said, rolling one about my palm. Thicker, a spiral design wrapping neatly around the white wax.
    'I found them near work. More expensive, but what

the hell. It's her birthday.' He gave a tired smile. 'Smell them. I think she'd like this smell.'

We come to the wall every year on Leila's birthday.

A karate teacher waddled a file of white-kitted children to an emptier stretch. Within touching distance of the wall they stopped and bowed. A woman in a sequined burqa was talking quietly with her daughters. One of the girls was in a purple headscarf with a scalloped hem, while the younger, perhaps not of age, was dressed in a T-shirt and tiered skirt. They inserted prayers written on scraps of paper into gaps between the bricks.

We brought out a plastic shovel from Riz's bag. Along the yellow scoop the plastic had frayed and turned pasty white. The shovel was part of a set we'd bought Leila before a beach holiday. It had a sticker on the bucket, of a bear sliding down a rainbow, that she'd pick at. We bring the shovel every year but it's too blunt, too flimsy for the dry, tight soil of this patch of cratered green, the real work is done with our fingers. Soon we had holes two inches deep. We stood our candles in the earth. Packed the cavities with soil. Twenty minutes we sat and around us a scatter of bent and blacked sticks grew as the wind time and again guttered the candles.

Everywhere else the stench overwhelms. It hits you in the stomach. No one seems able to do anything. Sometimes you see Slummers wading through the garbage, looking for things to sell.

A huge cheer went up. Two young men were visible above the thicket of heads, attempting the wall. They wore only white nylon basketball shorts with oilskin pouches tied at their chests, moving with upward pounces at unnerving speed, backs, calves, arms twitching and tensing, bodies bending double and right around like jackknives. One of the men was very dark-skinned. The other had a tuft of hair in the middle of his back. With the tips of fingers and bare toes they'd get a hold in the minute crannies and ledges between the uneven bricks, swinging higher all the time. The mob hummed with reverence.

'How strong, to leverage their bodies this way,' I said.

'It doesn't seem possible,' Riz replied. 'This sheer face. How are they doing it?'

'Why not. Like those guys who pull giant chariots by themselves with metal hooks buried into their backs.'

'Or the Shias. Whipping themselves to mush.'

The dark man tensed into a crouch and sprung to a jutting brick above. He couldn't grab on. As he fell through the air he hammered the wall with his fingertips, striking like a snake at its surface. On the fourth attempt the fingers stuck. His shoulder wrenched and his body twisted but he clung on with a soft, stifled cry. We exhaled as one. He swung like a pendulum from one hand, grinning down at us unflustered, until he found a niche for his other. Extending his legs, he swung them up over his head so now he was upside down, biceps bursting, lank hair falling in perfect glistening straights like granite rain. He took a foothold and pulled himself upright. Relief in the cheering now.

When I dream about Leila she is always in the distance, outside the light, but I know she has a warm, open face. I still see her eyes, light like my mother's, irises warm gold-brown pools in which the sun set ablaze radial chips of malachite, green and faintly black. She is impatient to meet the world, my little girl grown. She is taller than me. This makes me so happy. Sometimes she's in school uniform, walking toe-heel, toe-heel, back arched, the proud shoulders and strong nose of all the women in our family.

Today she turned nineteen. Desires, insecurities, angers that I know nothing of, though I must've played my part in. I would know so little about her now. Maybe her laugh. When she was an infant I'd bring my face right to her nose and make a funny sound – '*khwaaishhh*' – and she'd squirm with delight, cackling with a deep, cadent lilt. Her laughter now will carry a kernel of that. So I come here on her birthday. To ask her for forgiveness. We didn't respect these walls, so they took her from me. Sixteen years. Does she wonder sometimes where I am? If I abandoned her? I've read the books. She won't remember. She was taken on her birthday, only three years old, so she doesn't, can't, remember. When I think about this, it's like I'm burning on the inside. She wouldn't know me if we crossed on the road.

To her I am an emptiness, an ache she cannot understand but yearns to fill. No. I have left more, a glimmer at least. The blurred outline of a face. A tracery of scent. The weight of fingertips on her cheek. The warmth of her first cradle, my arms. I found a journal on early cognition in the library. One article said our first memories go back to two and a few months. We don't remember how things flow into each other, how they are linked, but our minds can place, in the vast fog, discrete islands. Maybe she remembers accompanying me to the mall one winter morning, white-frame sunglasses on her head. A Santa greeting the customers walking in. Leila so thrilled by this her shoulders began to vibrate. She squeezed my hand, still trembling, tugging gently until we stepped out of the security-check line.

I could see only his unfitness. Thin-limbed, dark-skinned, sweating in the hard noon sun. Over the double doors forlorn clumps of cotton glued to the lintel. Peach foundation trickling down his forehead like muddy rain down a window. But Leila was transported. She ran to him, mindless of the stale, cheap duvetyne, its acrid whiff. She was laughing and he pinched her cheek between his hairy knuckles. I didn't say a word.

'You want a present from Santa?' I finally asked. There were gift-wrapped boxes piled against the front window, clearly empty.

Leila looked confused by this. Maybe she didn't know what Santa did. The suit, the beard, an image in some book come to life, this was what thrilled her. The burden of age is expectation. It leaves a judging eye. She turned to me and smiled in a lopsided way, as if suddenly aware of her excitement, and when I saw her expression, that gentle glint, I felt her elation as if it were growing within me. Of course this place was enough. There was charm to be found here, there was nothing tacky. My baby's full-beam happiness at its centre, and I as innocent as her, as untroubled.

All this. Why do I fool myself? Leila will remember something quite different, if she remembers anything at all.

We gathered our things. The wicks had almost touched the ground. Riz's flame shivered for a few seconds in the wind and then gave up as well. I've come here every birthday since we lost her. There will be thirty-two candle stubs buried about this little lawn. When I find Leila I will dig up each one.

The dark man was struggling. This wasn't a race, the route up too tricky, still the air was fevered, an elemental rivalry. The men represented different lower orders. You don't see the high communities at street level very often, only on festivals. Around us garbage lay strewn, claiming the pavement, paper, matter, polythene fusing wetly into grime. In the shadows the trash had mounded and the long mouths of wandering livestock burrowed deep. The air so thick that with every breath I could feel a sediment, something black and gritty settling in my chest.

A wet yell. The other man had made it past the last of the handprints, only twenty feet from the top. At his knees gleamed the last red splotch. Fingers carefully splayed, the square palm defined. He made two more movements, rising a few feet. Holding on with his toes and one hand, this man tugged at the thread around his chest until the mouth of the oilskin pouch had loosened enough to dip his right hand inside. He pulled his hand out, holding a bright red palm aloft to wild cheers. He thrust his hand against the wall with a sense of theatre, pressing down from every angle like a rolling press. The highest anyone had gone. As the crowd continued to cheer he began the climb down.

The dark man was ten feet below, stuck. He cast about desperately for a gap in the brick face. Red handprints fanned out around him. This was as high as most got. The mob had shifted in mood. Some people began to hoot, which turned into a chant. Finally he lunged. From his slumped shoulders it seemed he knew he wouldn't make it. He grabbed with his left hand but clutched at nothing, seeming to bounce back off the wall, not falling along the face but arcing out, ever further from the bricks as he dropped. The crowd braced for impact. He fell directly into the mass of people. In unison everyone took a single step back, like ripples in a pond, and there was a sickening crack, a seamless *farrackfatfat* like the sudden spit of a log fire. It wasn't clear if the crowd had broken his fall, as it was supposed to. We turned quickly and walked away.

==

Riz died the same night they took our daughter. Yet here he is, by my side, as I walk from the wall to the huge field where our old school, Yellowstone, used to be. It's like this every year. On Leila's birthday he comes back, sharper here than anywhere else. He has grown old with me, my loving husband. This stoop and granulated stubble, the slowed walk, the dull coin of scalp showing at the crown. He was twenty-eight when he died. Why does he look older? Maybe I find him as I need. Maybe it is something else.

Tonight is auspicious, a rare alignment of moon and planet, star and node. There will be a display at the field too. We walked together through a parking lot and gully with overlays of political graffiti on either side before turning onto a main road. No one else walked here. It's the rancid smell, and the rats, big as cats, scuttling out from the garbage and scampering hairily over your feet. Most people take the long route. All the way down this road there is a dense, growing pile of trash that has shaped over the years into an incline covering half the street. Festering peels, thick trickles of fluid, unidentifiable patches of white and yellow, bulging plastic packets breached at the gut, oozing. Soaked, blackened rag-like emanations, long as dupattas, fished out from blocked sewers by scavenger-caste men who dive in little chaddhis into manholes. The smell was so bad we trotted, almost jogging, as we followed the curve of the road. Just then a huge grinding and crashing. A massive gate built in the upper half of the wall slowly retracted, joining the network of flyroads way over our heads. The wet amber eyes of passing cars blinked out in procession into the darkness.

Riz had his neck craned back. Still his jaw hung slightly slack. 'These flyroads are everywhere now,' he said. 'Throughout the city.' He pointed to a node in the distance. Three flyroads came together in long concrete sweeps, lifted to their magnificent height by grey pillars, broad and round, anchored deep in the concrete ground. 'They link into one another,' he said.

'How else will they get around? Can you imagine Dipanita or Nakul, any of our friends, if they had to see all this?

'"*It's so filthy down here!*

'"*I thought all this was over.*

'"*Must they bathe on the footpath like that? It's like they have no shame left.*"'

Riz's smile glimmered in the darkness.

I've never been on a flyroad. I've heard it's different to drive around up there. Easier to breathe. The air doesn't pick at your eyes, as it does down here, all day secretly seeping through your lids, by evening the rim around each eye inflamed. We turned a corner. For this last stretch no wall loomed over us and there was a glow in the sky like bouncing blue fire. Music; incantations set to pounding beats. The road ends at what used to be a large cricket field. You can still see half a burnt-down scoreboard with the Yellowstone crest and motto. Riz and I met in this school. This was where we wanted Leila to go.

Thousands of people stood on the old cricket field. People danced, prayed, sang and chanted, drums pounding, around small fires, a mad tumult that had something of the swell and fetch of an ocean. Motorbikes ripped up and down each zone with young men whirling the flags of their community. Yet one circle near the centre was almost empty. White velvet on the walls, white carpeting. Big cars coming off the flyroads arrived into this empty patch and as soon as each docked the driver leapt out. A family would emerge from the back seat and slowly, to show respect, walk the length of the zone to the stage. Once they had made their offering and touched the man-god's feet they walked back, climbed into their cars, were driven away.

The man-god, a gristly beard over a flowing gown, waistcoat of gold embroidery, stood centre stage, on either side ladies with thaalis in their hands. They had tied their saris low on the waist. As he canted into the microphone the women pulsed their shoulders. The music changed and they began to dance, bending at the waist from side to side, towards him, away from him.

'Is this it – the culture they wanted?' Riz suddenly asked. He is angry. He doesn't take heart from the search, as I do.

Moths and gadflies flutter into our faces as they race to the stage lights, dazed, convinced they'd finally found the moon. Wolf whistles cut through the electronic dholaks and rhinal singing coming from the elaborate arrangement of outdoor speakers. The top layer of speakers slicked blue from the stage lights. The audience dances on, thrusting elbows and crotches, clinging off one another and leaping about.

On stage, two dancers carried out massive wicker baskets. They placed them at the front of the stage and retreated to a safe distance. The audience started to throw metal objects at the baskets – copper bracelets, silver rings, earrings, necklaces, amulets, buckles. The outer sectors were competing. When the baskets brimmed with dull metal the man-god walked to the front and extended his arms. Everyone seemed to stop, a hush fell over the watchers, like a tablecloth that snaps in the air and slowly descends. Four men in black T-shirts emerged to carry the baskets centre stage. The man-god began to swing his arms in alternating circles, finding the rhythm, faster as the tempo rose. Thick arms whirred into a blur as the beat climbed. The air gathered up, suddenly thicker. Then the lights went off, only the purple glow from a cylindrical blacklight found the man-god's gold waistcoat, and at this the audience combusted, a hysteric peal that rolled around the crowd like the skirt of a dervish. The man-god stopped. Perfectly still, he let out a long, high yell. The lights came back on. Both baskets were filled now with gold.

The applause was deafening. As the four men carried the baskets off-stage, Riz shouted into my ear, 'All I can remember is how beautiful this place used to be. Coming here every lunch. I still see you in that school dress. That silly belt.'

Maybe we have the same conversation every year. 'Have I told you,' I asked, 'what I think of when we come here? The day I came for Leila's admission. We were lined up in front of that gate. It would've been there, where that man in the white shirt is standing – there with his legs crossed. It was so hot that morning the school windows shone like silver foil.'

'Wasn't this the long summer?'

'Yes,' I said.

I was nervous that day. I distracted myself by counting how many women waiting in line with me seemed to glint in the open sun. Their phones and fingers, earrings and oversize sunglasses. It was only mid-morning but a serious heat powered down. Dust devils roamed the parking lot. The birds were long gone, the trees naked of leaves. Everyone in line fidgeted as sweat sprang from awkward places. We weren't used to being outside. 'One by one, mothers and fathers trooped back,' I whispered to Riz. 'How scared I was when I reached the front. Running down the lists stapled to the bulletin board behind the gate. Then I saw her name. Two years, ten months. Your name alongside.'

'I remember that call,' Riz said. 'You were crying.' As he stared at the Ministry buildings in the distance he hooked the collar of his shirt with his finger and gripped it between clamped teeth, sucking in soft pulls. Suddenly I was exhausted, without the will to tug the cloth from his mouth, as I used to. 'We were going to give her everything,' he said.

Yes, we were. But Leila didn't have a chance to go to this school. She didn't get to wear the pleated blue skirt with the awful belt, tie a ribbon in her curls, show off the Caran d'Ache colour pencils her mother had saved for her since before she was born. Leila didn't get to study here but still we return once a year to this. It helps to imagine another thread, a tapestry of might-haves.

==

I was tired of slapping at mosquitoes. I turned to say something and Riz was no longer with me. He comes and goes as he wants now. Finding Leila is our quest, the last thing we will do together. That's why I always buy and bury two candles on her birthday, one from each of us. Riz will find peace when we find her.

'Nine o' clock. The badminton will be over,' I said out loud. I jammed the plastic shovel a little safer into my satchel and began the walk to the bus stop.

TOWERS

I am forty-three years old. A widow, living in a crumbling residential complex called the Towers. The complex was constructed near the southeastern border: head through the old city gates that look like a mouth missing its teeth, pass the landfill, the last stretch of the East Slum, the paneer-packing plant, the puffy silver-white tents of the tulip farms. When I first got here sixteen years ago the Towers stood in an empty basin of turmeric-yellow earth, the only relief in the vastness a row of factory sheds and the red and white stacks of a power plant in the distance.

I was twenty-eight when they brought me here, though I remember only fragments. Maybe it was the pills, Dr Iyer's pills, that left me in a muddle. Some people have reported palpitations, night sweats, a sudden inability to breathe, but the pills have helped me. I take one every night even now.

My first nights here were warm and airless, so hemmed in that each breath felt difficult, as if a large man was pressing my face to his chest. Through a crack in the curtains a column of blank blue night. Blue light lining everything in the room. Like an invalid I examined every corner of my new home, one-room-kitchen-attached-bath. The ceramic and metal door handle. Peels of paint where seepage had furred one wall. The flimsy brushed aluminium of the stove. The cabinet for the gas cylinder was slightly warped and the door, which did not properly close, made a woody report against the frame every few minutes, making my heart jump. Riz and I were married five years. We were together, in all, eleven years, save one break of almost a year. How love changes. We were so alive, so needing of each other at first. Over time the sex became perfunctory. Our attention shifted to our daughter. When Riz and I fought, I could imagine Leila and me casting off together, better off without him. But I knew even in my anger that there were comforts I drew upon every night. The rhythm of his breathing. The peculiar smells his body issued. The way he reached for me, racked by a dream. Suddenly, for the first time in many years, I was again by myself. My bed felt too big, solitary, a seclusion, as if I'd committed a terrible infraction and my in-laws had sent me back to my parents' home, to spend my nights alone, unloved. That was how little I understood then; how young I was when I first got here.

Most nights I could not sleep. After hours of fidgeting I would climb from the swelter between the sheets, find the small jam jar I keep in my purse, pop the thick rubber seal and swallow down a blue and white capsule with a glass of water. Only then would I return to bed to wait under the fan.

But they work. This little pill will turn the mind from the vigils of the day, the memories we guard, the images we polish and protect and return to. Leila's wide, crooked smile. Riz holding me from behind in bed, safe as a swaddle. The scything ache between my shoulders wanes, memories billow and contract, now everywhere there's a slow, warm tingle. I'm staring at something soft, something smooth, a sheet of white satin that ripples in a wind, and drawing towards it, I see there's no distance between my self and these folds of satin memory, we are one, the same.

The pill gives three hours. Three hours to coast on a smooth straight road glowing in the sun, to recover strength, find sleep. By three-thirty a familiar dream. Asleep in bed, my own, my lost bed, I can smell faintly the potted lavender that helps Riz's apnoea, when there's a small shift of weight underneath me. I sense from the way the mattress has rolled that Leila has climbed in. Something must have scared her. I open out my arms so she can slide between us. Her chicken-bone arm will now fall to my breast, her shoulder press into my ribs. I reach for her. Then I reach again. I cast my leg about but there is only empty coolness. Remembrance is an alarm, a siren that plies round my head. Gone, she is gone. There is no more sleep. I plead with the ceiling for rest as the room brims with light. Through the rift in the curtains the sky is brightly blue, a smear of empty cloud. All the while Leila floats above me, the broad bridge of her tiny nose, brown-green eyes a touch too far apart, a pert, trusting smile. She is pinning my shoulders. Stifling my breathing. I have to jump, fly from this cursed bed.

==

Leila had a way of copying me.

The first time I found her doing it I felt this surge of hot love. A sense of ownership, but more than that. *I belong to her as much as she does to me.* Tears began to come down my face. When she turned and spotted me, she looked so worried that I ran to her laughing and we held each other. I can feel even now her arms on my neck.

Winter, because the air was thick, grey light, purifiers pumping in every room. A few months before she was taken. Leila had gone into my bedroom and peeled off one of the bindis I kept stuck on my dressing table mirror. It looked enormous between the down of her eyebrows.

She'd taken a dupatta and a pair of low heels from my cupboard. The dupatta went over one shoulder of her sleeveless sweater like the pallu of a sari. Her fleshy feet with toes like white tulips reached only halfway up my heels, but she was walking with confidence, an unsteady, willing traipse up and down the living room. She'd seated her dolls on the couch and when she reached that end of the room she scolded them with a wagging finger.

Even as that wave of warm pleasure filled me I worried: Did I shout at her like that? When?

==

I was introduced to the pills at Purity Camp. When I first got there I felt in pieces, a solitary step from the brink, ensnared by the wide, open fields with the lonely gabled sheds. But I wasn't crazy, I was clear about that. I did not rave or run about naked. I did not raise my voice in anger. The pills helped. There were other ways to cope. Many picked up odd little habits, anxious for routine. A bee that fights its way out of a beer first performs muddled rotations of the mug, looping wider and wider in the afternoon air. That's what all of us were like at Camp. Doing desperate little things so we could remember what was normal.

One of the inmates kept her distance from the rest of us. She wouldn't say a word during meals or before bed. The girls called her Lady Police, a name that immediately stuck. This woman had a cascade of fine white hair, though a young face, nose and jaw still sharp, skin unlined, under the thin kurta-pyjama the smooth, fitful thrust of an athletic body. Lady Police did not walk; she'd stride about the place. Every morning and evening, at about the same time, she would strike out from the dormitories, past the playing fields, towards the scant groves that stood on the eastern edge of Camp. There was, always, something forward, something purposeful in her gait. She hardly spoke to another person but it seemed without question that she was going somewhere, as if important work was at hand when in reality there was nothing to do. Every day it annoyed me more. One evening I decided to follow her.

Dusk had bruised the sky cobalt and purple. A wind shook the branches of the jujubes and lifted skims of yellow dust into my eyes. At first it was easy to follow her because many women walked about the cooling evening, but soon there were only two of us, and I had to hold back, until the distance went to fifty or sixty yards. By the time I entered the grove she was nowhere to be seen.

I walked in wide ovals, searching against the ash-grey silhouettes of bush and tree for the bob of her white head, until there she was, sitting in the mud alone, cross-legged, upright, her back to me. I had to stop short and retreat in an arc, crouching behind the mottled trunk of a young peelu.

She awaited company. In front of her was a plate, a knife, a fork. Four place settings had been arranged. The flatware had been filched from the dining room. I should've been angry, because we faced shortages of everything, but out here that did not matter. Lady Police sat calmly in the soil. She would nod, smile, turn her head to the plates around her, mutter for a few seconds, take the tumbler to her lips like a child playing at a tea party.

I can't tell you how long I stood there. I had started following her with a sense I was doing something wrong. Now the guilt was overwhelming. I knew that I had grabbed at something special – repeated the plunder that had brought us here. I turned and ran, scrambling through the dead leaves. Most evenings I watched Lady Police leaving for the grove. I even talked to her a couple of times, but I never let on.

==

Riz's corpse was likely burned and dumped in a gutter in the sandlands on the eastern edge of the city. Hundreds of men were left there, those who spoke against the summer's madness. Riz fought so that Leila wouldn't be taken. Me? I will die a coward, submissive to the last. Out of confusion. Because I'm scared. Alone. Because this is the way now. I have many excuses. When they brought me here they gave me a job at the Revenue Ministry. Slummers did the wet swabbing and collected refuse. We were to perform peon duties, take papers around, dust the desks, keep the appliances working. Tea for the senior officers. Open the triple-decker tiffin boxes, serve lunch, wash the plates and glasses and receptacles. Unslept, I carried a dozen cups of milky sweet tea on a thin aluminium tray, shuffling between offices, sectioning out sugar or buying milk or scrubbing the film of orange oil from aachaar containers. The hours were long, the commute terrible. Exhaustion accompanied me where I went.

==

Most nights I would toss in my bed for hours. This one-room apartment was another chamber for my brain, a larger casing from which each thought bounced its way back. So I walked. I'd slip out of my building and follow the mud track the shuttle buses used to take us to work, walking until a pink smudge growing in the distance split the night into land and sky. When the sun came up I would all at once feel the tiredness, the ache in my calves and feet, and turn around. These night walks helped me understand my new home better. By day all I saw was stubbled flatland, but night sharpened my awareness of the smallest inclines and descents, and under each step I could sense an ancient, subtle topography. It was on one of these night walks, just as it was turning to winter my first year, that I saw the young boy.

A sharp, moonless December night. Everything around me very still. The ant colonies like craggy cliffs, in the distance silver trees with spectral tentacles. I had only a thin jacket so I held my arms tight across my chest, hands warming at my pits, walking quickly. This mud track is elevated, two feet higher than the farmland on either side. Once this was wheat country, but the farms were abandoned during the water crisis. By the time we were sent here nothing grew but grey-brown scrub. A pack of mongrels leapt out from behind a stack of bricks on the side of the road. They stopped barking when they recognised me. The leader, with handsome haunches and a white tip to his tail, came to lick my hand. I was glad of their company. You saw snakes twisting across these roads sometimes, their scales left a faint sodium slather on the tar. One at a time the dogs turned back to their territory, the last whimpering softly as she went. That was when I heard the steady, flat report down the road. Thup. Thup. Thup. We each hold somewhere within us the expectation we will be safe. A sense of security is our abiding illusion.

No longer, not me. Each person must construct their own inviolability, fashion it from the things they find. My daughter had been taken precisely because I could not protect her. I put my hand in my pocket and felt the warm wooden handle of the switch knife I carried in my jeans. I had practised, in front of a mirror, twisting it into an attacker's inner thigh, the blade would go in smoother there. I rubbed my forefinger against the metal flick switch and felt a surge of confidence. Even two men I could handle with this in my hand. The flat rolling emptiness helps. A car can be heard kilometres away. When I catch the chesty whine of a Wagon's engine I stop walking, and as soon as the beams from the headlight begin to bounce down the path ahead of me I step off the track, slide down a couple of feet to the soft, loose earth.

Now there were no headlights, only this thup-thup-thup carrying out from the well of blackness behind me. It seemed to be moving fast. From somewhere the long blare of a train. It stopped, then started again. I got on my ass and turned to lie on the dry mud bank on my stomach. Planted years ago to break the invading wind that hurtled through the crop and partnered with the sun to set off ruinous fires, the poplars had each been shorn by the long summer. They grew along the side of the road like giant besoms jammed into the mud. The earth was cold against my blouse. My knees and toes sank into the bank. A biting wind came in from the east, low, sweeping through the dry grass like a thousand slithering snakes. Thup-thup-thup. Then, unmistakable, sobbing, a young voice, muttering reassurances around each smoky breath. The boy was not more than twelve years old. He wore under a sweater a kurta that the starlight streaked silver and blue. His hair was turbaned, the knot low on his forehead. I waited as he jogged past. Before he was lost to the darkness again, I shouted, 'Wait, child.' Sneakers scuffed against gravel. Silent now, he studied the darkness behind him.

'I can see you,' I said. The wind grazed my cheeks like shards of glass.

'Who's there?' he shouted, a puff of steam rising from his mouth. 'Show yourself. Where are you?'

'Don't run.' I clambered up to the road. 'Don't worry.'

He backed away as I walked towards him. Already tall, a slight squint to his eyes, on his cheeks and jaw, down halfway his neck, long curls of hair. He took a proper look at me. 'What are you doing out here?' he asked.

'I'm asking you that. You live around here?'

'I had to run.' He wiped his face with his wrists, and, placing two fingers on a nostril, blew his nose sharply into the dirt. A kara bounced down his arm. 'Mummy-Papa made me. Those men came to our house tonight.'

'We need to get off this road, child. They'll be coming any moment. What's your name?'

'Roop.'

'Look here, Roop, will you come with me?'

He nodded. Taking him by the hand, we walked to the hiding spot, where we rested with our backs on the mud bank. Grey clouds raced one another against the dark sky. The rhythm-rattle of cicadas. The boy slowly regained breath and composure, his hands between my palms.

'Who came for you, Roop?'

'The Repeaters. They came to our house.'

'Why?'

'My neighbour . . . he's fighting with Papa.'

'What about?'

'They always fight. Every day.'

'But who called the Repeaters?'

'My neighbour,' the boy said quietly. He wiped his face with the shoulder of his shirt. 'He knew my mother is from another sector. He said my parents lied.'

A fat, brown lizard trundled by, bloated from the bounty in these dead fields. It stopped by us, looked around and flicked its tongue. The lizard's beady gaze reminded me of someone I could not place, a face from Camp, or the night the Repeaters came, a reptile fat on sadness. The boy was crying again, his yowls high in the air. A matter of time before they heard. I squeezed his shoulder and drew him closer to the lizard. The wailing stopped as the boy's face scrunched in confusion. We were now so close the creature must have felt our breath on its back, but it didn't move, it seemed not to see us at all. The boy stared at the scales, like tiny dragon wings, along its flanks. Out of my reach lurked the memory of that angular face, jaw, nose, the insatiate darting eyes. Quick as lightning I landed my palm on the lizard's back. It squirmed and fought, tickling my flesh. I held it by the stomach, squeezed it of its life, raised it to the boy's face.

'See, nothing to be afraid of.' My voice was so calm. 'Survive. That is the important thing. When they are fat and slow we will get revenge.' I could feel him trembling. I tossed the lizard into the fields and we watched the limp body arc into the night. 'What will you do? Do you have a place to go?'

'Can't I go with you?'

I rubbed dirt into my hands to dry the lizard's secretions.

'No.'

'But why?' he asked, drawing the second word out, a longing in his tone that made him sound, for the first time, truly a child.

'Where I live, children aren't allowed. Especially not children like you. We have Wardens. They'd take you away.'

'No children? Where are they?' Roop asked.

'We should get moving,' I said. 'Not together. Stay on this road. Move quickly, quietly. In about thirty minutes you'll come to a crossing by a huge dumping ground. Be careful you don't fall. The road becomes very tough to walk on. Take a left at the crossing. When you reach the power plant, look for the sheds for the labourers. They'll take care of you tonight. Don't tell anyone what you told me. Don't mention your parents at all. If they ask, say your family had gone to a rally and you got lost there. Okay?'

'I can't go alone, Auntie. I'm scared.'

Again that note of ache, of yearning. I wanted to wrap him in my arms, keep him safe forever. Instead I said, 'You have to go now, Roop. Your parents will come looking for you. They must be able to find you.'

He turned to me with a curious, pinched expression. The scraggle of hair on his chin no longer danced with fear. He swung a leg up and was onto the road in an instant. A furrow appeared on his forehead. He seemed about to say something but then decided against it, and I had the unsettling feeling, from the way he looked down, that to him I was no different from that lizard. A chasm in my gut as he jogged away. It felt like I'd just retched. This hairy, dirty boy, so many years older than my little girl. I hadn't spoken to a child in months. One moment the boy was leaning on me, breathing heavy, his whimpers throaty and wet. Then he was gone.

I sat sunk in that loose gravel it's hard to say how long. The wind burned against my chest. I huddled into myself. Then I heard the Wagon, a giant SUV, enamel-white, flags rippling in the slipstream. The driver leaned on the horn though he steered the only thing on the road. My perch under the road felt secure, warm. I lay face-front against the mud bank again, watching the headlights swing from side to side, occasionally sink or rise, growing steadily until each blue beam was like the iris in my eye. All the while yelps and rabid howls from the men hanging out the windows, poking out the sunroof, drinking deeply from a plastic bottle filled with booze, intoxicated by their sudden primacy.

I wonder sometimes how the boy is. If they caught him that night and took him wherever it is they take our children. Why didn't I sit with him a while longer? Only a few minutes more and the Repeaters would've gone right past.

Him too I did not protect.

==

Leila had her typhoid booster. She was brave about the injection, but I knew the inevitable tomorrow – small kicks under the bedsheets, breath like coal dust in her chest, fluttering eyelids, the heat in her arms. I took her from the pediatrician to a playpen on the ground floor of a new mall. Between the inflatable slides and a large bungee swing, a train with red, yellow and blue carriages, making beeps, whistles, soft chug-chugs. A slender man in striped overalls and hat watched the sides of the train from the back while another drove. Children waved when they went by their parents. Giddy expressions as they were carried away, on some faces furrows, momentary panic, the anxiety of separation written sharper.

Leila wanted on the train at once. We walked up together when it halted but the conductor rose from his seat in the rear carriage and waved his flag angrily until I stepped back. Leila wrenched her arm free of my grip and hopped onto the carriage, claiming a spot on a bench by the window. Her sudden movement surprised me. I must've stood in that spot for a few seconds, clutching at the air. When I turned around a woman holding a little boy by the hand was smiling at me. I looked away, embarrassed, but later smiled at her. I wanted to say, I'm proud, just look at my daughter.

Tiny hands clenching the apron of the window for balance as she stared at the silvery shop-fronts, unperturbed by a pair of boys squabbling behind her. The driver took the train around an island of potted plants, and then I could see her properly once again, a bit confused, shivering with excitement. When she spotted me a light seemed to fill her face, a huge smile erupted, and then she was pointing at me, clapping, bouncing in her spot. The way she looked at me. I was filled with a golden warmth. Replete. She and me together, the track, the circle.

Now the memory of Leila's face is like a skewer. Jiggling pigtails, bright shopper's lights, the green eyes twinkle. A sudden deep smile because we had come together once more. Her need for me, mine for her. The memory burns, takes me forward through these days like a goad in an elephant's neck. Our eyes will meet. When I see her she will smile like that again.

==

Warden Khanna and I sat with the others watching a middle-aged pair take on two younger women. Wafts of spoiling milk from a ground-floor apartment. The four darted about the court: grunts, racquet whips, sneaker screeches.

'Do you know, Shalini, they were the ones who built this court,' Khanna said.

'Who did?'

He pointed to the older couple. 'Ms Poonawalla, Ms Dwivedi. Do you know them?'

'Yes, of course. Nice ladies.'

A serve sailed into the air. Orange sky streaking to purple. The taller of the young women bounced in the backcourt, coiled to smash, but at the last underarmed a return. Dwivedi was ready, leaping up as her racquet whistled from high over her head, pushing the younger women to the edge of the court, where they began a frantic grunting defence, bent low, a soft tock springing from the racquets each time a desperate arm retrieved the shuttle inches from the concrete. Whip-smash-ungh-tock, whip-smash-ungh-tock, the saves bringing gasps from us watching. One of the young women deftly dropped her hands, and this time the shuttle looped to the forecourt, where Poonawalla had watched the exchange with her racquet poised, thrumming, eager to intrude. She took three side steps and went so hard at the shuttle that it caught the tape and bounced back to her feet. She screamed out a curse. Some of the women giggled.

'Usually they are nice,' Mr Khanna laughed, shaking his head. 'Padmini takes her badminton very seriously. She used to play before she was brought here.' He had an air of sheepish self-importance. 'They came to me for permission to put the court up.' Khanna leaned back, flexing the legs of his chair until the red plastic joins whitened under his weight. I wondered if they would suddenly snap. 'I only got them the net.'

'I remember two women making the chalk markings. They were so serious. Measurements in a little notebook. Their tape rule. My god, so much time has passed. Look at them now.'

Khanna patted his belly and smiled. 'They look quite fit to me.'

'Of course, of course,' I said. Another sharp smash and the cork of the shuttle cracked loudly on the stone. The younger women slapped hands. In the surrounding towers tiny squares of light popped into life.

The years have passed slowly. Outside it is difficult but here good women try to rebuild their lives. This badminton court is one thing we have. They string up lights on the poles that hold up the net. By dusk the rest of us come down, someone organises tea. At first I never went down in the evening. It seemed so strange, grown women playing the games of children, of men, but I've come to appreciate it now.

'What's this I'm hearing, Shalini, that you aren't happy at work?'

'Who told you that, Wardenjee? That's not true.'

'Then why did you apply for a transfer?'

'Oh that.' It's still a surprise that Warden Khanna knows so much about my life. How does he keep track of every woman in the building? 'I thought it was time for a change.'

'Change?' Khanna turned to look at me. Lines ran like a rainbow across his forehead, so deep they looked cut with a knife. 'You know the Council doesn't like that. We have to stay where we are. In the work we've been given.'

'I've tried two or three times before.'

'Yes, I know. They told me that this time you'll go before a tribunal.'

'I'm not afraid.'

'You're not?' He sat half-twisted, like a lemon, staring into me. Does he know I've worked towards this transfer for sixteen years? He pushed himself to his feet. 'That's up to you, of course. But be careful. These tribunal people have many powers. Okay, Shalini. Come over one of these days.' He put two fingers of his right hand on his heart. 'Purity for all,' he said.

I put two fingers on my left breast, eyes on the badminton. 'Purity for all.'

MA AND PAPA

A single clear memory of what it was like before, though I must be four years old. My parents are taking me to lunch at a new grill at the Sheraton. I'm excited, dressed up, nervous. We travel to the top floor in a mirrored elevator. Even this is something new, and I remember the reflection it presents: the bunched folds of Ma's sari, my favourite headband, baby blue with rows of white polka dots. The elevator opens into an oak-panelled vestibule where two hostesses are waiting to lead us through a curtained door to a restaurant floor warm with sunlight. I let out a little gasp. A picture window along one wall offers a flowing view of the city below. I run to see. The treetops are different lustrous greens, gently swaying and leaning into one another. Even Ma is surprised by how many trees there are. I press my nose to the chilled glass. A toy city, overgrown with broccoli. Through the leaves you see houses, white or yellow, small rooms on their roofs. It is the sight of the trees that stays with me. A trembling canopy over the city, properly broken only in a few places: a crop of office buildings, the stadium, the domes of the medieval monuments, each cupola shining smooth as a beach pebble.

Some forty years after Purity One was erected there are no trees. The stunning canopy is gone. Now there are hundreds of walls, no one sure how many. Each wall is fifty-nine feet high and two feet thick, in agreement with Council law. They loop through and around the city, bigger than anything except the tallest buildings. My father detested these walls. Now that I use the Outroads every day, I live with what they expel. I must see their shit and slime, the cascading brown water and showering refuse. Smells so thick you can taste them. When children fire bottle rockets over the walls of their sector, trying to hit the Slum roofs, smouldering dregs of fireworks come floating down on me as I'm walking. If a load dumped from a trashtower comes gush-tumble-bouncing down a sector wall, the warm, gritty splash carries to the other side of even the widest road, leaving a rain of brown drops on my shoulders, my hair. Papa was right. These walls diminish us. Make us something less than human. Go out of the city, to the low hills in the west perhaps. Look at this place at night. The silent grey walls and between them the flyroads thrumming with headlights. We are in an enormous maze.

A hundred years ago the city's first wealth settled on Lakshmi Hill. Rice merchants, factory owners, or, like my great-grandfather, builders for the British, raising the new city. My father grew up on the Hill, in a ground-floor apartment with a long hall that his cousins and he used to race tricycles down. Bedrooms one side, kitchen and living room the other. He married a pale, pretty nineteen-year-old from the Wadhwa clan in the front garden, with champagne and a jazz band. My mother gave birth to me in that apartment. We only lived there until I was seven, but till the day I married my home was always the Hill. There were so many things to love. Going barefoot up and down the cold marble steps leading up from the portico. The high ceiling of my room. French windows that opened on to our own lawn. The cook's cubbyhole behind the kitchen, where I would sometimes hide, where it smelt like incense and, faintly, mattress mildew. The fuzzy bear ballerinas I'd stuck in their different poses on the doors of my cupboard, staring back at me even after we'd emptied the room.

One summer, while we were still in that apartment, Papa, Ma and I went on a walk. A dark evening, with a cool, crackling wind such as there is before rain. Papa swung angrily at a cloud of mosquitoes that hummed over his head. He nodded to the other walkers. He had biscuits for the mongrels. Once upon a time, he announced, the cigarette vendors and dervaans would salute as we walked by. He pointed out the trees, the sharp, sour smell of the toddy palms, the cloying aroma of the figs, bittersweet tamarinds, the acidic coconut smell of the banyans. My father taught me to recognise the trees that grew there by their smell.

I wanted to race my mother down the road, but she swatted my hand away. 'That woman has been digging through our trash again,' she told my father.

'What's wrong with her?' As Papa spoke his neck flushed into two patches of pink. 'Does she go through it herself? She's that crazy?'

'I've caught her doing it. Now she brings a servant.'

'You know how rich she must be?' my father said, shaking his head. 'Looking for bones! I've never heard anything so crazy. What does she do when she sees you?'

'She's bloody brazen. Doesn't care. She kept rooting through it, saying, "Nothing personal, dear. Try and understand." I knew I had to keep cool. So I told her – very politely! – "My husband's family has been in this building sixty years. We're an old family. A good family." She was totally unmoved. Kept saying – in this calm voice – "Of course, of course, I know you're not just anybody. But the rules have changed. We have our own habits. There's no need for there to be such a fuss. We simply want to live with people who follow our own rules, from our own community." "So we have to go, is that it? So you go through my trash?" I asked. To which she replied, in that infuriating deadpan, "Madam, you know the rules. Rules were changed with the building society's permission." "So

you're getting rid of us because we're not the same caste?"
You should've seen how horrified that bitch was,' Ma said.
'Her eyes went really big. "Caste? No-no-no-no-no. How
can you say this? There is no such thing any more. This is
only our community. We want to keep our homes pure.
Our surroundings." I wanted to hit her.'

We walked past an idling truck. From its uncovered stern
a lean, sinewy man polished like teak by the humidity
arranged gooseberries in the pannier perched on his wife's
head. She carried each load to a row of fruit stalls on one
side of the road.

'Why didn't you?' my father said with a laugh. 'Might
have made it worthwhile.'

'Will it rain? Should we turn around?'

'No. It's not going to rain,' Papa said.

It was the same story all over the city. What we put into the
body is so personal, intrinsic to family, belief. No politician
dared argue against walls built around food. Purity came to
have different meanings. Some people wanted no meat at
all, some would eat only fish. In other areas Muslims were
evicting anyone who drank alcohol or ate pork. Once a
community had control, its society revived laws written by
colony builders a hundred years ago, ensuring land could
not be sold to those who did not belong.

==

In the living room of that garden apartment we had a gramophone with a brass horn. Next to it a waist-high Ganesha. Against one wall was a rolltop desk I could never open without a struggle, and on top of this a rotary telephone sat. When I was about four or five I had a game. I'd put the barbell-receiver to my ear and rotate the dial, in turn from each number, starting at the satisfying spiral of clicks at nine and finishing at the abbreviated twirl at one, in between each rotation pressing down on the nipple-like disconnect button again and again to listen for the ding from the other end.

One afternoon I was pacing about the living room anxious to play this game. Ma was on the phone. She was facing the wall, as you had to while using this instrument, leaning forward with an elbow on a fat phone book. Perhaps she was already upset. My only interest was getting to the phone. Was I buzzing around her, worrying at her, urgent in my need to resume this game? Or was I further back, striding up and down the long living room, tummy turbid with longing, when she slammed her palm on the phone book? It made such a thump I jumped back. 'Will you fucking stop!' she shouted. Her voice bounced back from the corners of the room. I was terrified. But I can't even remember now if she was yelling at me or into the phone, at Papa or someone else.

==

With the money for the flat my father bought a white stucco house in a neighbourhood that was bisected by a sewer. We left there within a year. The next one I hardly remember. Localities were self-enclosing. Papa seemed to age each time we moved. Increasingly, he looked beaten. He died eleven years after we left his childhood home, never taking his evening walk again. I was angry, but now I'm glad. He went before the eternal order took root, found the fissures and crannies, pried us apart like volcanic rock.

One evening we three were watching the news. He was on his armchair, Mummy on a bench, while I lay on my stomach on the thick rug between them, flicking through a textbook. I must have been in my teen years by then; I remember being aware that this was a novel way of delivering the news, no longer the solitary monotone, resplendent moustache or starched stiff in sari, instead four or five people crowded around a table, this new breed of newsman at the centre, conductor of the cacophony. One of the studio guests, a thin, bearded man, was shouting into the screen. 'Real estate listings have become like matrimonials! Brahmin-only, Yadav-only, Parsi-only. Is this the way they want us to live? As if we must be separated, like fighting children?'

Papa put his drink down and leaned towards the screen. There was a change in the air in the room, a sharpening. My mother looked up from her crossword.

On screen, a frail, paunchy man rapped on the table. I had noticed him at once because he looked like my Indian music teacher, wearing a white kurta and dhoti, and rectangular half-frame glasses he'd derisively polish whenever anyone else had the camera's attention.

The anchor was now deferential, his plummy affect withering. 'Mr Joshi, you have the floor.'

Joshi cleared his throat and went immediately into a tirade. 'Who are you to criticise?' He looked directly into the camera, speaking to the viewers, gently establishing the other's inconsequence. 'These intellectuals think they know everything. But I know, I know, they are thinking only about Western values. They show no care for our own values, how we have always lived. Don't go by these foreign ideas of what is right, what is wrong. This is our way of living. There is nothing wrong. It is the flowering of an ancient consciousness.'

The bearded man made some sort of interjection, making my father nod and grunt, but to me his words seemed pallid, forceless, of such little weight that they escape me altogether. He was given a handful of seconds and then the newsman, recovering his vaguely colonial accent, called upon Joshi once again.

'What has the government done all these years?' Joshi shouted. 'Nothing at all. What-all people coming from everywhere. Where are they coming from? What they are eating? Sleeping on the streets, in parks, underneath our new bridges, doing their morning business right in the gutter, gutters where there is no water. Good people are getting angry. The anger is palpable, I tell you, palpable! This is our chance. We can free ourselves, at last, from these ghastly visions.'

'Why do we have to watch this every night?' my father suddenly shouted, convulsing for an instant, knees jerking up, palms going to his temples as if the discussion was painful to his ears. The remote was with him, the question rhetorical. Still both Mummy and me were quiet, scared of adding to his anger. We watched as he landed finally on a showing of film songs from the fifties and sixties, coiffed heroes, black and white, the angular beauty of the actresses further pronounced by the ageing film stock, and this seemed to slowly soothe him; wisps of remembered rhythms, the memories they brought forth, first infatuations, first tremors.

==

Under pressure from my mother, Papa relented and bought a two-storey home in the Arora Pavilion. I remember my disappointment, the first time we drove into the neighbourhood, because we didn't have a Purity Wall. I'd never seen one up close. All the girls and boys in my class had been taken by their parents to see Purity One. This made me even keener to go. But my father was adamant.

One afternoon, as Papa was driving me home from piano class, we had to take a detour because some of the roads had been cordoned off for a Council convoy. Papa slumped low in his seat. I was reading a book and ignored him at first, thinking he was trying to be funny – he had slipped so low that his shoulder bumped against the gearshift as he stared upwards, beyond the windshield. Then I saw it myself. Gunmetal grey and shining in the sunshine, darkening much of the road with its giant shadow, like something from a movie, an alien ship settled. I had to slide down so I could see the top of the wall. Papa couldn't focus on the traffic. Each time he looked at it he made these soft clicks with his mouth, saliva emerging in mercury spurts. He swerved across three lanes of cars, parked in the last, and jumped from the front seat, grunting at me to follow.

I caught up with him when he was very close to the wall. He slowly moved closer, neck craned, placed his fingertips on it and gently pushed. I ran to the wall. Smooth stone, wonderfully cool, like the granite floor of a temple's sanctum. I put one cheek to its surface and enjoyed the descending shiver. Papa looked sunk in thought. He said, 'You go one hundred steps that way. I'll go this way. No more, okay? Come straight back. Run. Let's see how far this wall goes.'

As Papa walked away he trailed his fingers on the wall. I headed the other way, walking past a group of European tourists who were taking photographs. I realised the wall was following an indiscernible curve. After a while I stopped, struck, all at once, by just how enormous this was: either side of me the serpentine wall stretched off into the horizon. Later, as I walked back to my father in the lee of this enormous thing, I felt an overpowering urge. I stopped again. When there was no one in sight I measured out a little more than an arm's distance from the wall. My eyes closed and arms spread wide, I began to twirl in a tight circle, gathering speed, pounding my foot against the asphalt, once with each spin like a kathak dancer, enjoying the sudden breeze against my face, chest, arms, freedom from balance and position and sense, eyes screwed tight even when the giddiness became too much and I had to hurl myself back-first against the wall and it was hard to tell now where the wall ended and ground began, as if the level world had yielded and everything swayed like a ship rocked by wild waves. I was submerged, backed up against it, for delicious seconds slumped in that high. Slowly a sense of calm returned. When I came to, the beads of sweat on my upper lip and temples and forehead were gone, a nip coasted the air.

Papa was walking in a frantic oval exactly where we'd left one another. 'I found a gate!' he said. 'Why did you take so long? I want to check it out.' A muscle had begun to twitch just above his right eye. He took my hand. The gate was black, solid metal, twice my father's height, cordoned off by a red and white boom. Half a dozen men strewn on plastic chairs, heavy wooden sticks by their sides. White vests showed under cheap cotton shirts opened to the heat. They spoke in lilting drawls, making casual injuries to each other's mothers and sisters.

As we watched, the three rows of metal spikes on our side of the gate withdrew into the road. The rope-man heaved and the barrier sprang up as the gate opened and a long car came through. Beyond the gate neat, narrow roads, pavements of pale pink kota. Next to the road a pathway for pedestrians. A line of one-storey houses with handkerchief gardens and a sudden current of heathery fresh-cut grass from a park where children my age swung and slid and chased each other. A small temple. A wall of gleaming brass bells with strips of holy cloth tied to the clappers. Papa made for the pedestrian entrance. He gripped my hand so tight the bones at the flanks of my palm wrenched. Our forgotten car, which he'd parked by half-jumping onto the pavement, was at the tip now of a snarl of cars and bikes.

Two men leapt to their feet at our approach. Only one walked towards us, a long wooden stick in his right hand. The street lights had just come on, their filaments unnerving behind the big glass cases, like the glowing, trembling antennae of a rank of cocooned insects. 'What do you want?' he asked, unsmiling.

Papa returned his grimace. 'We thought we'd take a look inside.'

A smirk. 'This is the Patel sector. Only Kadva Patels inside.' He looked at us closely. 'For non-residents . . . you have permission? You will need permission.' He walked to a shed built like a phone box, with gaps between the wooden slats, and looked through the cardboard container they used as a drawer. He came back with a form in his hand. 'Fill this out and mail to the office. They will see.'

'You mean I can't go in just now? My daughter and I can't just walk in?'

'Get permission,' he shrugged.

Papa made a familiar movement, shoulders rising sinuously until his back was straight and he was standing his full height. 'Who are you to tell me where I can go?' my father asked. 'I go where I want! This is my city.'

This time no mistaking the smugness. 'Go where you want, Uncle. But not here.' A wet, mocking chirp of commiseration. 'Don't worry. Get permission from the elders. Then who am I to stop you?'

'I don't need permission. From you or your bloody elders.'

The other guard whispered something into his mate's ear and they both laughed, blocking the path shoulder to shoulder. 'We protect our people from what-all goes on outside,' the second guard said. 'Filth in air. In character.' Two fingers of his right hand went across his chest. 'Purity for all.'

Papa was so disturbed he couldn't stand still. 'Purity for all? Have you gone crazy, all of you? Who told you this was allowed?' he screamed. 'That you could do this to my city?' At the raised voice, the other guards jumped up from their seats, plastic legs grating against the concrete, and ran with short, quick strides to us. They formed a semi-circle around Papa. I realised with some surprise that my father was not a large man. His wrists were slender, sleeves flapping around his biceps. The crop of white hair added to his frailty.

'Stay over there, Shalini. Stay over there.' He turned back to the men. 'You think I take orders from people like you? You're going to tell me where to go?' The men were angering. One, who looked like their leader, smacked his stick on the ground. Each time it came down with a splintering sound.

'Who are we? What maharaja are *you*?' this man growled. He placed a thick finger on my father's chest. 'What's your name? Which sector are you from? Why are you coming here?' Rapid questions each culminating with a prod in the sternum. My father went bright red. He twisted the leader's collar into his fist and put his other hand on the man's shoulder and propelled him backwards, so quick the others didn't move. The Repeater kept balance, flailing, for a few steps. When he went to the ground he took Papa with him. He rolled my father around and pinned his shoulders to the pavement. He slapped him hard across the cheek. A slim scarlet line appeared just below the eye. I screamed and ran towards them but someone, the first guard, scooped me off the ground. He held me by the shoulders as I tore at the air. The other guards had surrounded my father now. They pummelled, kicked, some used hockey sticks. In my panic I couldn't hold a thought.

'Calm down, calm down,' the guard was whispering. I opened my eyes. The beating had stopped. The Repeaters stood around my father. His face and neck were spattered with blood. The top buttons of his shirt had popped and salt-pepper chest hair showed. The guard put me down and knelt so we could look eye to eye. 'We could do much more. But he is an old man. Confused. Get him out of here.'

'Yes. I will,' I sobbed.

'If the elders saw what happened they would make us punish him properly. If they had seen, it wouldn't be in our control.'

On the drive home, the cut under Papa's eye puffed like a paperweight until he couldn't see. His arms, back and chest had blue and coffee-brown streaks. When he lit a cigarette in the car, hands still shaking, a narrow black welt showed on his forearm. After this day we stopped talking so much. The ease we'd shared all our lives seemed to evaporate. It wasn't all his fault. Maybe I avoided him too. Those guards handled him as if he was nothing more than a nuisance. I could no longer look at him in the way I once had, impervious, invulnerable. He probably saw that. Saw me. An ungrateful, unthinking daughter.

CENTRE OF HIS PALM

The Yellowstone school bus was a dust-striped rattletrap. On winter mornings it emerged from the fog with two giant eyes square on you. The seats had filth written across their backs and always felt damp. The floor revolting – anything you dropped green and grimy in seconds – though with a pretty pattern in aluminium in parallel tracks down the aisle. Mornings we were all subdued by the day ahead but the afternoons were better. By a quarter to four, when we got on the bus, the heat was dimming and the wind had picked up, and a sense of abandon washed through the air.

Some couldn't properly handle the few minutes we idled in the parking lot. There were squabbles, little ones crying, fist fights. A teacher with a printed list checked off names as we formed a loose line around her. There was a tall, curly-haired boy from a year above, a poorer kid, you could tell that right away, his uniform faded from extra washing, cheap shoes. This boy with the heavy curls jumped aboard and ran to the back, tossing his school bag to claim the long back seat, the white Rexene fraying with slashes from compass points and dividers. He shouted something out the window, combed his hair back with his fingers, began to pulse his pelvis in tandem with an ally on another bus. This sort of behaviour was what the teachers called 'filmy', 'roadside', 'cheap'. Certainly not acceptable. But the teachers waiting to climb on board with us ignored him. They were like that at this time of day, sinking into the front seats as if they'd been switched off. By the time we were on the open road there would be water bottle fights and bra-snapping. Long-term couples would retreat to the back. Some boys would wrestle. The forward ones would swipe the scrunchies from our hair, stick their hands out of the window, threaten to release them into the wind until we begged.

On some days the din became too much and the junior school art teacher, Mr Basak, was sent to quieten us. An old Bengali, losing his hearing, touched by Parkinson's. One afternoon Basak came lurching down the aisle. A boy had pulled the white casing at the top of each seat a few inches up so that when Basak clutched at one it would collapse uselessly in his fingers instead of steadying him. Twice he stumbled. The old man was furious, his glasses opaque, a pair of frosted windows. We shook with silent laughter. He threatened to involve the other teachers. Then, a few rows down, a boy with his hair slicked into a middle parting popped up above the seats like a prairie animal. 'Woil ou please sayt,' he shouted, and ducked. Basak whirled around dangerously. Through our years in school we'd made fun of his Bengali accent, thick rolled vowels and dropped consonants. Hearing this good-looking boy copy him, I was holding my stomach, tearing with laughter right in front of the old man as he repeated, 'Oo said thees? Oo said?'

Riz was a year above. I'd seen him look once or twice as I walked down the bus aisle. Maybe he liked how much I enjoyed his joke. The next day he took the three-seater just in front of me. I was playing a game with two girls from my class. You put down the name of a boy next to your own, cancelled out the letters that were common, this was supposed to tell if you were destined to 'love', 'hate', or be 'friends'. A film song played over tattered speakers. The smell of a leftover lunch being eaten. I was cutting letters out with practised speed when a voice broke in.

'You should try it with my name,' Riz said. He was up on his seat on his knees, arms wrapped around the top of the backrest.

'It's just a stupid game. For kids,' I said. I was annoyed at myself. There was a greenish tinge where his skin had been inflamed by a razor. He smiled coquettishly, like a movie star. Strong sunlight through the half-tint windows left amber shimmers in his hair. Through the rotting speakers the song turned to a wail. As he spoke he flicked his middle parting into place, a movement that sent a warm thrill down me. A pencil moustache made his jaw a perfect square. Maybe it was his unhesitant admission of interest, unusual at that age. I felt instant hunger.

We did try the game. The result it yielded escapes me. He displaced the two girls next to me, surprising me by pulling a harmonica out of his bag and putting it to his lips. Then he shook his head and slipped it into his breast pocket, saying, 'I'm trying to learn.' My hands were flat on my thighs, and I was aware, suddenly, of how grimy my elbow pits were. Rubbing them with a finger left grains of oily dirt, like eraser dust. When he wasn't looking I rolled the sleeves of my shirt down. Everything happened so fast, just as I wanted the bus to take the longest way home it could. I talked about the essay competition I'd entered. He told me about the squash team, that he'd spent most of the summer playing one-pound video games on the 'awesome' machines at the Trocadero in London. 'That's a lot, like fifty rupees. But the games are much better than they are here.' He'd learnt to drive already, he said. Just before his stop he took my number and wrote it in his notebook, the last page, covered in scrawls, stalemate noughts and crosses, doodles of *Archie*-comic-shaped girls. I was sure he wouldn't call.

He did, that very night, so late that my parents were asleep. At first it was awkward. Then he told me a secret:

a friend from the squash team was two-timing the most popular girl in their batch, a cold-eyed stunner called Radhika. I told him about a chubby girl on our bus whose ancient math tutor would lightly rub her nipples between his forefinger and thumb, shivering all the way through their one-hour sessions. That was how we went, bartering confidences until the sky started to glow. From that first night it felt warm and natural.

A few hours later, on the bus, I took the window side of a two-seater, blocking the adjacent seat with my school bag in anticipation. He walked by me without a glance. Was that a smirk? I was mortified all the way to school, alone in a double seat, unsure he would join, sharply aware of each spent minute. In school I stewed all day, picking apart what I'd said last night to find something wrong. But in the afternoon, without acknowledging the morning, he once again left his friends and scatted my companions away. The night's intimacy came rushing back. We held hands. I used my finger to trace circles in the centre of his palm, as a friend had taught me. He squirmed, closing his eyes. We took the turn for Nizam's Abode, the Ashraf sector where he lived. Just before his stop, by a billboard with a girl in a sparkling hijab, we kissed for the first time.

By then my family had settled down as well, in accordance with the new way. Living inside the Arora sector left you with a subtle – not always unpleasant – feeling of enclosure. As soon as you passed the gates you felt them looming behind your neck. The walls were visible almost everywhere. Papa had found a narrow two-storey in a line of identical homes with pocketbook gardens and fez-like red-tile roofs. From my bedroom, looking out to the east, the wall was two hundred metres away. It hung over the spread of little houses with the placidity of a mountain. From the sliding window in the living room and the parental room directly above it the wall was more than a kilometre out. Still you could see it in patches, though most of this side was obscured by a manmade hill on which the richer families of our community had constructed their mansions; you'd see it again, behind the segmented white shikhar of the Shirdi Sai Baba temple; in the northwest, standing sentry beyond the succession of soccer and cricket fields. After a while I hardly noticed, and coming home felt like you'd been brought back somewhere safe, tucked in, paddocked.

For months I tried to hide the relationship with Riz from my parents. Then Ma said one day that she could hear my phone ringing every night through the paper-thin walls of our new home. She promised not to tell my father, but at dinner some weeks later, Papa told a story about Riz's dad, gossip from the club. Riz's father and other garment exporters had bribed key bureaucrats to keep the rupee below value. Grubbing is typical of exporters, my father said suddenly. It was strange, because Papa never cared about my friends or their families. I don't remember him mentioning Riz again.

Summer arrived with a loo wheeling in every day from the western desert. The wind rasped like sandpaper and left a smatter of maroon spots on your skin. School broke a week early because two young children dropped with heatstroke. Riz and I planned to sneak out to a movie, on a Monday, because that was when Ma had a long lunch with her college friends.

A stifling noon, a pale sky, flat as a bedsheet. The glare seemed to bounce from the whitewashed stone houses. Papa was at work, Ma at her lunch. From my window, while waiting, I saw a blue and white slipper melt into the surface of the road. The phone was ringing. It was Riz. 'Just made it,' he whispered. 'For a second there . . .'
   'What did they say?'
   'Fuckin' assholes. Your Repeaters are really hardcore, man. The worst.'

Riz explained on the phone. As I'd been waiting by the window, he and his brother Naseer were driving up to the main gate. Naz was one year younger but liked to say that his brother was the one who needed protection. 'Bhai is not a fighter. He's built for love.' Riz told amusing stories of his younger brother's gang, eight or nine hulking bodybuilders in skullcaps he'd gathered up from one of the low-income gyms in Nizam's Abode. Naz called them 'his back'. He would say to me, with a small boy's earnestness, in his slingshot sentences, 'If any guy, *annny* guy, says or does anything to you. Inside your sector even. I don't care. You just tell me. I'll take care of them. I can do anything for Riz. Means I'll do anything for you.'

At the gate, the Repeaters had circled their father's new blue-grey BMW sedan. One Repeater stuck his head in Riz's window. 'Get out.'

Riz and Naz emerged from the car into a hard, high sun. The two- and three-storey homes in the distance jiggled from the heat vapours climbing into the air. The parks were empty at this hour, a row of aluminium slides glinting with venom.

'ID,' the Repeater said. Riz handed over the ID he'd bought, willing his brother to remain calm.

'Kushagra Arora,' the man read, his face wrinkled up. 'But how is it I haven't seen either of you before?'

Perhaps it was only the young ones, wilful about love, who faced this problem. The best schools had not yet been transplanted, fields, auditoriums, all, to whichever sector that could afford to buy them. Boys and girls from different sectors were thrown together all day. Students devised all sorts of ways to deal with the Repeaters. Yellowstone had a peon named Raju whose job it was to ring the bell between classes. One of the senior boys discovered that Raju knew how to forge. For twelve hundred rupees he would give, in three days, a workable rendition of the ID you needed, your photograph on it. Each sector had its own caste insignia, distinctive edges, signatures, backgrounds. The tricky part must've been the watermark: the pyramid and, underneath that, 'Purity for All'.

'We usually come in from Gate 4,' Riz said. 'Our house is that side.'

'How come we've never seen you before?' Naz said, forever belligerent. 'How long have you been working here?'

A worried look crept onto the Repeater's face. 'I've been here almost six months.' He raised the ID cards to examine them better. 'You both are living in the Crescent?'

'Yes,' Naz said, taking a couple of steps forward. 'Are you even allowed there? Or do you have to hang around out here, by the wall?'

The Repeater handed them their identification. 'I'm sorry about this. I didn't know you were in the Crescent.'

'We're one of the first families,' Naz went on, enjoying himself now, even as the Repeater began walking away. 'What do you think? Our Abbu is on the committee.'

The Repeater stopped short. He whirled around, confused. 'Abbu? Did you say Abbu?' he called out. Another from the gang came up to him now. 'You heard, Rakesh? What this boy said? Can a boy from our community call his father such a thing?'

Naz looked from side to side, unable to move. Riz ran around the car to his brother, standing between Naz and the advancing Repeaters.

Riz put on his biggest smile. 'Look, boys, what're you saying? You want my brother to show you?' He opened his belt buckle and jammed his right hand in his jeans, taking grip of himself. He laughed now, with the men, back to his brother. Riz knew how to use his shoulders, his smile, the physicality of his charm. 'Or you want me to show? I can also. But if my mother found out you had checked her boys at the gate to see if they were cut like . . . like some boys from a madrasa . . . We would have to call her an ambulance, my friends.'

The second man was laughing. The first still looked suspicious. He closed in on Riz until there were inches between them, hovered, took a nearly imperceptible whiff.

'Look, boss,' Riz went on, 'I'll tell you the truth. I took this one out to teach him to drive. He thinks he's old enough. Maybe. Now I'm not sure he's smart enough.' A smile cracked the second man's face. 'We didn't tell our father we were taking his new car. I don't want to tell him like this, calling from the gate. You understand, don't you? Papa has a really bad temper. First he'd be angry with you, then we would face his full anger. Here, let me give you something for tea. Don't say no, take it, take it. We're brothers, after all. Just don't tell our parents, okay?'

Riz's phone call disturbed me deeply, touched a nerve that I knew would be twanged again. Even at that age I could sense it. By the time Riz reached my house I was in tears. The servants were asleep in their quarters so I went to the door myself. A blast of heat took my breath away. I pulled him inside and quickly shut the door behind us.

'Why are *you* crying?' he asked, annoyed, but he wiped my cheeks with tender fingers.

'I'm sorry.'

'It's not your fault. Don't cry.' He was staring hard at the ground as he paced around the coffee table in our small living room. 'I'll sort that guard out,' he muttered. 'Smelling me. Like I'm an animal. Who the fuck does he think he is?'

'*Smelling* you?'

'You know it wasn't even that.' He stopped walking and looked right at me. 'It wasn't what he said. I had to lie today about who I am, where I'm from. It's humiliating.

I'm not ashamed! But I had to lie just so that . . . just for . . .'

'Just for me!' I shouted, dismayed. Hot tears again. 'You can say it. Just for me.'

He came to the doorway, where I still stood, wrapped his arms around me. I put my arms around his neck. He thrust me against the wall. For minutes we kissed in the living room. Suddenly the realisation that a servant could walk in any time. 'Do you want to see my room?' I asked. 'But where is Naz? We can't make him wait outside. Let him come in.'

'Don't worry. He's gone roaming with the car. He's never been inside a sector like this. He wanted to see what goes on.'

When we walked up the stairs Riz pinched me through my Daisy Dukes. My room was dark and still cool from the morning's AC. With a toe I flicked the heavy, green switch, then a couple of lights. 'So much pink!' he laughed. 'It even smells pink.'

Too much for us at first, that sense of open possibility. Hands clasped behind him like an inspecting sergeant, Riz walked around the room looking at the assortment of posters and photo-spreads from rock and Hollywood glossies. I used to double-tape them to the walls. He took three or four circles of my room as I sat on my bed, shifting my legs from under me to the floor time and again. It suddenly dawned that he'd gripped his own hands to keep them from shaking. The next time he came close I caressed his forearm. The hairs stood on end. Then he was by my side on the bed and we were kissing. Then he was on top. *A servant walks in now and Papa will never speak to me again.* The heat and weight of his thighs felt good around my waist, lips roamed my neck, his teeth strained at the collar of my T-shirt. My room was suddenly a different place, the metal-frame headboard looking strange upside down, the sweeps of brass between the corner posts now like a ship's railing, the pink curtains and walls with a deeper, fuller, velvet cast. Every inch of me – the girl who would cut Sellotape into little rounds and carefully attach six pieces to each photograph – someone else entirely. The bra came off. I let out a long, low moan. *Would he tell his friends how I moaned? His brother, on the way back, how smoothly he slipped my bra out from under my shirt?* Riz shuddered in response. He was tugging at my shirt with his teeth, teasing it off so he could concentrate on my breasts. *Panic.* I grabbed his wrist and said no. He looked up with a big grin, eyes wide and hungry. Then he went back to inching it up and off. My fingers were wrapped around his wrist. I tightened my grip, smiled and shook my head again. Don't do that. I watched his powerful shoulders. He looked at me again, smile gone, confused. Nothing's wrong, I said, I just can't take my shirt off. He laughed and wanted to know why. For many minutes I refused to explain, as he nibbled at my breasts and my ribs, sure that I would yield. When he didn't stop asking I had to explain. Innocent of where this afternoon would lead, I'd forgotten to shave my underarms. Very sweetly, Riz spent the next two hours in my bed with his tongue and mouth wandering between the hem of my shirt, which was pushed up around my neck, and the waistband of my shorts. He kissed me for a long time through my denim shorts, making me spin, roiling my sense of control over my own body. Later, when we spoke on the phone, Riz laughed that I'd moaned and thrashed like a fish out of water. I made fun of the look on his face when he first saw my breasts. By then both of us were nervous about how needy we'd been.

In school we saw each other during breakfast and lunch breaks. Once in a while we found an empty room. Most of the time it was footsie under a library table, holding hands. On the bus we took the back seat, tucked away by one window while another couple occupied the other. I sent him home every day swollen to burst. Sometimes I could feel wetness surrounding the bump in his pants. I masturbated as soon as I got back from school. That second year together passed quickly. Riz, in his final year, had permission to take his car out late. I'd spend the night at a friend's place. Just before he graduated we began to have sex. We went in big groups to dingy bars where smoke hung in torpid swirls by the ceiling and the management didn't care about sector rules or the drinking age. We went to nightclubs, long rooms with green lasers arrowing through blackness and bathrooms made entirely from mirror and granite.

We nearly made it through the four years Riz was away in Oberlin, but he stayed on campus his last summer, asking for '*some* independence'. I wondered why his emphasis was on the first word when in truth the second was operative. One year, he said, then he'd be back. I was angry but decided to wait. I had a sense from movies of what college in America was like. Sitting in my room, at my new computer, seeing his username brighten when he popped online; determined not to initiate contact; losing patience, affecting a casual tone in some unnecessary message, simmering, a few minutes later sending a link to a song I'd been listening to – is he there? No response. Watching his name fade to grey as he went away without saying hello.

I graduated from college that year, English honours. A couple of weeks after graduation I got drunk one night with some friends and slept with a long-haired design student called Jethro, real name Jaiveer Arora. He'd given me a ride home on his motorbike. An awful experience, sneaking through his parents' bedroom, his own room stale with smoke. I avoided him all summer. A rumour spread in our sector that I was a slut.

That September my father died. A year before we were told he'd contracted emphysema, which they diagnosed as linked to COPD. He wasn't able to work. This made him shrink further into himself. My mother gave English tuitions to young kids who lived around us. Papa sat on a rocking chair. Even that sometimes was too much and he'd become short of breath, wheezing as if his ribs had collapsed, his chest sunken in on itself, then gasping furiously. He coughed up a grey-green mucus throughout the day, sometimes with such force that a blob would land a few feet away in front of him. Clear liquid slowly spreading across the tile, separating from the viscidity at its heart. Ma so distraught. I cleaned up after.

Ma had been lonely for a long time. Me too, without realising it. Then Riz came back. He had just returned from America. He'd never met my father but he rushed to our house as soon as the news spread. Riz talked quietly for half an hour with my mother as she sat glaze-eyed on a long straw mat someone had placed on the floor of our living room. He left right after with a thin smile in my direction. When he returned he had a framed, enlarged passport photograph of my father under his arm. My mother started howling. As it went up on the wall she insisted no one would garland it with marigolds.

Riz came every day, served tea and snacks to the visitors. In the evening we'd go for a walk. This was the only time I could cry. His shirt would be soaked at the shoulder. For the first two weeks an aunt and two cousins slept with my mother and me on mattresses in the living room. Riz stayed every day until bedtime. He would tell my cousins silly jokes as they helped him spread the bedsheets across each mattress. Later he told me he had to bribe the Repeaters week by week to allow him into the sector, that they were more understanding because there'd been a death.

I wonder what Papa would've made of my wedding. The nikaah was on a January morning in the family haveli in Riz's ancestral village, surrounded by the family's mango orchards, two years after Papa died. Mummy and Dipanita, my best friend, came. We left at dawn in our old light-blue Fiat. The driver couldn't keep up with the convoy and soon we had turned down a village road with low whitewashed houses and grocery stores and tiny photo studios on either side, as men sitting by the side with white beards and orange hair tucked under skullcaps stared into our vehicle, curious about the city women. Mummy and

I were getting angrier. The driver's brain seemed to have suddenly switched off. The road narrowing all the time. I was afraid, though I couldn't bring myself to say it, that one of the front wheels would suddenly descend into a gutter, making us even later. A village autorickshaw, the kind that can squeeze in eight or ten passengers, came down the opposite way. We tried to go around but neither could advance. I started shouting, mad at Ma, at the driver. Dipanita making soothing sounds from the front seat. Finally I called Riz. As soon as I heard his voice I started crying. He gave precise instructions. We reversed down that narrow road, coming to a small roundabout. Naz appeared fifteen minutes later, by which time I was so furious at our stupidity I was ready to go home. He was in a 4×4, one of his cousins beside him. He scrunched up from the wrong side of the road, wheels spinning out an orange cloud of dust, flipped his Oakleys to his forehead.

'Shall we, ladies?' A huge smile as he looked around. 'Nice spot you've found. But maulvi-sahab is waiting.' When he saw my expression his face changed. 'Why so upset, Shal? Ammi, Abbu, everyone is relaxing at the house. The maulvi's having a great time. He's drunk three cups of tea, straight from the saucer. Quite a sight. Quite a sound too.' He grinned when I laughed. Then he turned to my driver. 'And you. Keep up this time. I'm watching you.'

The haveli got no sun that day. After our apologies were dismissed I was rushed to a narrow tube-lit room where my mother helped me change. Riz was in the living room with the men of his family and the maulvi. The open-air corridor that led to them was filmed with ice-crunchy-dew. Ma hissed at me to hitch up the jaal gharara they'd given: *don't let it get spoilt.* We were led to an adjacent room with thin white mattresses spread over every inch of floor. Silently I repeated the name I'd chosen, 'Yasmeen, Yasmeen, Yasmeen,' after the Disney princess.

Ma seemed to like Riz. She didn't make a fuss about his father's insistence on a nikaah. They found a maulvi who would look the other way on conversion. She enjoyed herself in the haveli. After I assented to the maulvi's two or three questions, mumbled in Urdu, Mummy, Dips and I were suddenly in the centre of a gaggle of women, Riz's aunts and cousins. Riz walked in and they all started squealing. He seemed different in this house, more confident, though I'd never felt that lack in him before, broad and strong in a maroon salwar-kameez, hair leaking from the snug knitted white topi. He put his arm around my waist, which led to prodding and teasing, Mummy and Dipanita quick to join in. Photographs with a carousel of cousins, the younger ones shy. From the way they stared, maybe one or two had a crush on Riz.

Riz's uncle entered. Chachoo managed the family's land. Without saying much he took Riz's hand, escorting the two of us to the upper floor and down a veranda-hall that overlooked the gardens. The morning had refused to warm and I was shivering by the time we got there. He lifted a narrow wooden block that latched the low doorway at the end of the hall. Once he'd got us in the room, he pointed to the bed, eyes firmly to the floor. 'Take rest here,' he mumbled. 'Someone will come up in half an hour.'

We were in a damp room where high, shuttered windows let in slits of grey sky, the wooden bars on the windows so worn out they rattled in their grooves. I found a box of yellowing switches tacked to the wall. A tube-light sputtered above a steel almirah. The thought of fucking in this eighty-year-old haveli while my mother and his parents drank thick, milky tea below us. Dipanita sitting with them. I laughed silently. Carefully, I removed two layers, laid them on a chair, stretched out on the bed. Riz tossed off his kurta and joined me, both of us smiling at the way our families would treat us now.

Riz was fidgety on his back so he laid his head on my breast. His breathing got heavier. I was dropping off myself when he said, 'You know, my parents must've done it in this bed.'

'Well, yes. That's why we're here. Time to ravish Jasmine, Aladdin.'

'Really? You have the energy?'

'This room is freezing. And I have no idea how to get the rest of this thing off.'

'Abbu was probably too embarrassed to tell Chachoo about us. That we've been together.'

'Why on earth does your dad know that?' I asked, hitting Riz gently on the back of his head. There were cracks in the ceiling that looked like the nostrils and eyes of a small, crooked face. 'I wish Papa was here,' I said.

'How's your mum? Is she taking all of this okay?'

'Yeah. Lot of excitement. She looks pretty happy.'

'I'm glad. I was worried it would be too much.'

'No, no, she liked all of this. She was worried before.'

'What do you mean?' Riz's muffled voice was now alert. He rolled away from me and propped himself up with his right arm under his ear. The wind snapped a shutter open and a square of sunlight appeared on the bed, lighting up the dust mites around Riz's head like soda bubbles.

'Nothing, really. It was something she said.'

He didn't say anything, staring with a strained smile, arm bent into a neat scalene, thoughts racing behind his eyes.

'Baby, don't misunderstand,' I said. 'She was just being protective. I'm her only daughter. She's bound to be worried.'

Again no movement but the same tight tone. 'What did she say?'

'We opened a bottle of wine because it was my last night in the house. She's all alone now. But you know how much she likes you, right? She'd never say anything like that.'

'What was she worried about?'

'Oof. She just asked if I was sure I knew what I was doing. It was more like a joke. She poured us our second glass. Then she pushed her specs up her nose and said' – I tried to copy my mother's nervous delivery, hoping it would ease the tension – '"Riz is . . . he's *such* a nice boy. You know how much I like him. He was so helpful when your Papa passed away. And I know he's been there for you. I'll tell you, the biggest relief is that he's so different. He's not . . . typically Muslim, you know. Only thing is, sometimes they become very religious later. There is a tendency. Happened to one of my friends. Her husband became a fanatic late in life. Remember Leena Auntie? Daughters had to wear that hijab. The sons only allowed to marry Muslim girls. Imagine. Though their mother was a Hindu! I felt so bad."'

Riz seemed unoffended, amused even. I pulled him back to my breast. 'I've heard that before,' he said. 'Not from your mum of course. We must explain to her what a fanatic is. Was that it, then?'

'Yeah, pretty much.' I ran my fingers through his hair. 'She was worried you might suddenly decide to marry again. And again. "They can have four wives. Then what will you do?"'

'My poor baby. The night before you got married? What a mindfuck.'

'I told her I'd make you so miserable you'd never think of marrying again. And I will!'

His parents insisted we spend the night in the old house but while the family napped after lunch we took one of the drivers back to the city. Our school friends were waiting at a suite Riz had taken at the Claridges. We didn't have the typical drawn-out celebration because it was already complicated, our getting married. It wasn't against the law, but they made you feel like you'd done something terrible. Our photographs had to be displayed on a bulletin board at the police station for a month before our wedding. Reams of paperwork. Signed permission from both sets of parents on all kinds of forms. We filed photocopies of Papa's death certificate with seven different authorities. We had to declare a domicile. The rules were so strict that it was impossible now to live in his sector or mine in any kind of peace.

That was how we came to the East End.

WATER

I

We moved to the East End on a cloudy July morning. Riz's father refused to come down. He sat cross-legged on his bed, playing game after game of Patience. I stayed at the doorway when Riz went in. Abbu stared intently at his game, knitted brow, scowling. Riz stood at the foot of the high poster bed as his father refused to look up, neither saying anything. Movie songs on the transistor radio, the steady snap of plastic cards proficiently placed, gathered, shuffled. Finally Riz turned around and walked out. He looked like his father, the sullen furrowed forehead, an expression of irritated anger, of injustice. When we were in the hall, the bedroom door closed, I took Riz in my arms. He was trembling.

As the mover's truck was pulling out of the driveway his mother emerged, watching us from their grey kota porch. Riz got out of the car and went back to her. He held her by the shoulders, speaking quietly. When he waved a hand – Naz drumming on the steering wheel, eager to get going – I climbed out of the back seat and went over. The narrow folds of skin on Ammi's face and neck were wet with tears. I bent my head to her shoulder and she pulled me close, whispering in her broken English, 'Since he was a child Riz did what he wanted. He doesn't listen. Don't blame yourself.'

'We'll be back all the time, Ammi. It's very close. You know how much he loves you both.'

But his father didn't want us to come to the house any more. After all the shouting of the past weeks, now he was determined to silently seethe.

His wedding gift to us was the plot of land adjacent to the family home. Naz was to get the plot on the other side. Riz sold his without telling any of them. He bought a four-bedroom apartment in the East End. I'd never heard Naz speak angrily to his older brother before.

'Can't you see what you're doing to them?' Naz was driving fast, braking suddenly, darting into gaps in the traffic.

'What's the big deal?' Riz asked. 'It's not like we're leaving town.'

'It's the East End, man. Why are you going to that place? You know what it's like.'

'*What* is it like?'

'Everyone knows. Drugs. Women. It's godless, that place. Is that what you want? And what about us – the family? What are you doing? Tell me, is it her? Is Shalini making you do it?'

A hot flush of shame. I'd been uncomfortable in my short time in Nizam's Abode. The gentle fretting about my clothes, deemed 'too much for the area'. The strange, cloying smells. Teenaged servants fresh from the village, shy but staring. The tethered goats I'd seen all over the place in the weeks leading to Bakri-Eid, slow-blinking, oblivious, then suddenly all gone. Next day a crimson wash in the gutters. But I felt anger at Naz's question too. Maybe Riz had done this for me, but I hadn't asked for it.

'Are you insane, Naz?' Riz shouted. 'Don't piss me off. Just drive.'

We went past the high wall of another sector in silence, all three edgy, hackles up. Now the walls were everywhere. In ten years they'd appeared like a malignancy all over the city, as if the water pipes bubbled with this septic lymph. When we were approaching the East End gates, his voice calmer, Riz said, 'It's all these new rules, Naz. I can't live like that and neither should Shal. No booze, no pork. Old men with nothing to do but count how many times a week you go to the mosque. They want to send her to Koran classes! Can you imagine? It's a joke.'

'But everyone is doing it. Live with your own. Follow your own rules.'

I loved the East End. People liked to say all sorts of things, but in reality it was quiet and green, with a serene, unruffled air, as if nothing here had ever changed. There were parks, a mini-market, a health centre in the windows of which, driving past at night, you'd see a glowing double rank of Lycra-clad runners. Each bungalow had a front lawn, the narrow roads belted by the canopy of peepals, mango trees, flame of the forest. Regular speed bumps so the children could cycle. The residents had long ago decided against putting up a sector wall, everyone could come and go. It was strange to see a boundary wall like this now. It looked abbreviated, or rather undone, reminding me, in an unnerving way, of a desolation I'd seen upon a hillside as a child, an ascendance of blackened half-trunks, a forest of felled trees.

Naz was the first to mention it, as he pulled up at the East End gate. 'It looks so weird, doesn't it? Not having a wall there? Like they started but suddenly lost interest. You're so exposed.'

'Don't talk nonsense,' Riz said, but he had a curious expression, almost guilty.

'You can see the tops of the houses,' I told Naz. 'The first and second floors. It took us a bit of time too. You get used to it. And just see what beautiful trees grow here.'

The guards at the gate waved us through with only a cursory look.

'They took the decision as a group, all the neighbours together,' Riz explained, as Naz got moving again. 'That's what I like about this place. Everyone gets to decide. Not some old fuckers hiding behind Purity One.'

'Bhai, what was that poem they used to make us recite

in school?' Naz asked. He put on a deep voice, and taking one hand off the steering wheel, began to stroke an imaginary beard. 'Into that heaven of freedom, my father, let my country awake.' He started laughing.

We all smiled at the memory, morning assembly, bleary-eyed in the central courtyard just as the sun was coming to strength, cantillating the great man's verse without a thought to its meaning.

'So you found it finally? This is your heaven? Haven, maybe.' He laughed again, turning to me. 'Like you Punjabis pronounce. Haven of freedom.'

'Well, it's better than anywhere else,' Riz said, smiling. 'We just want to live our lives in peace.'

But Naz wasn't done. 'And in this haven of freedom, can I ask, what need for those guards? Why do you need those gates?'

'Tch. That is completely different,' Riz said. 'And you know it. It's always been like that.'

'What's different about it? Why did the guards let us in just now? Imagine if we had come walking. They'd be so happy to see us? Imagine if we were dark, disgusting from spending our lives on these rotting roads. You think they'd let us in?' Perhaps Naz sensed the drop in mood inside the car. I could not see Riz's face from the back seat, maybe Riz looked annoyed. 'Look, do whatever makes you happy. Who am I to say? I'm only sad that you're leaving the house. You both.'

Our apartment reminded me of my home on the Hill. Big bedrooms, the cold marble floor, a large picture window in the living room that looked out over a park. I read a lot by that window. I began contributing lifestyle pieces to a newspaper's weekly supplement. Leila was born our second summer. Riz would leave work earlier to spend time with us. Mummy came often, always with a matte silver box of kaju barfi.

I remember the morning Sapna, Leila's ayah, entered our home. Leila was three months old. We'd had a torrid time with servants. The night nurse was competent, expensive. We figured a month would be adequate. But since then had come one trial after another. One girl left in the middle of the night after some nippy remark I made. Household in instant disarray. Then came a middle-aged Bengali both Riz and I liked. She made our lives easier almost at once, we began sleeping full nights again. One afternoon she told me she wouldn't work for us any more. She wanted to go home to her village to spend time with her own growing children. Later I found out she was ensconced in a nearby sector. We had gushed about her to many people in our circle, the relief obvious, and she was poached by the friend of a friend.

Sapna was brought to the house by the cook of a couple we knew. They were relatively new friends, a gallerist and his wife. The wife did some work with poor women, I believe, helping them make and market saris. The food at their house was spectacular, even the foreign stuff, asparagus wrapped in prosciutto, things like that, and our friends were very proud of this cook, who was a dark, big-eyed, confident young thing. One morning they sent the cook to our door with Sapna.

By the time I got there they'd already been let in by the servant who answered the doorbell. I wondered for a moment how that was – neither this cook nor Sapna knew the people who worked at my house. But there is some code they have between themselves, and an understanding of circumstances, both ours and their own; the cook might've explained that Sapna had been brought here to fill a gap in the household, and the servant would've known then not to make them wait outside, that the first meeting went better inside the home, granting a dignity that standing supplicant at the door did not.

They waited in the kitchen. Sapna was looking at the ground, shoulders hunched, one hand resting on the granite counter and the other tucked behind her. The morning light from the big window framed her with a static-shimmer; golden rays seemed to be jumping from her skin in little volcanic bursts. As I walked into the kitchen Sapna seemed to shrink. Her shoulders hunkered further, she went lower, taking three or four quick little steps back until she was behind the woman who'd brought her here.

'She is from my Slum, didi,' said the cook. 'She's a very good girl. Aren't you?' she asked Sapna, turning to her.

Sapna remained silent. The top of her head and bent neck were clearly visible, but she seemed to think, as a cat does, that obscuring her own eyes would leave me unable to see her.

I let out a small laugh. 'There's no need for that here,' I said. 'Come out now. There's really nothing to be afraid of.'

'She doesn't say much, didi,' the cook told me.

'I can't have a mute. I need someone who can speak.'

'Come out from there!' my friend's cook said, impatient suddenly, yanking Sapna by the forearm so she seemed to roll out to view. 'Please give her a chance. She had a very tough time before this.'

The gallerist alluded to this when we spoke. 'What do you mean?' I asked.

Still Sapna did not say a word. She was frail, cocoa-skinned, with a high, gleaming forehead, her oiled hair pulled back tight. 'The madam at the old house, where she used to work, she was very bad.'

'What did she do?'

'Her husband was in Railways. They promised Sapna's

parents they would get her a job, but she had to work for them one year without salary. Government job is best, didi. You get lifelong salary, pension, room to stay. Her parents sent Sapna to the couple. Just thirteen years old. For three years they did not let Sapna leave the house. They did not give her salary. She had to take care of two children. One was only a baby. They made her do everything, cleaning the house, cooking.' She grabbed her by the wrist. 'See how thin she is. They hardly gave her food. The madam used to beat her with things, jhadoo, stick.'

I felt a deep anger then, at these people who take advantage of the poor, who make it so difficult for the rest of us, who would never do such things.

'Come here, Sapna,' I ordered. She looked so young. When she was in front of me I put my hand to her cheek. "There is nothing to be frightened of, okay? You don't have to worry about anything like that here. Do you know how to take care of children?'

'Yes, I do,' she said. Her first words, so low they were barely audible.

'My daughter Leila is a baby. Only three months old. You know how to take care of a girl that young?'

'Yes, didi. I have done it before.' The sound of her own voice seemed to give confidence. 'Whatever you tell me I will do.'

'Yes. She's a very quick learner,' the cook chimed in.

'This I've seen myself.'

'No one will hit you here. And you will always be paid. Every month you will get your salary on the third. All our servants get paid on that day.'

She looked up at me, eyes grateful, somewhat baffled, her expression retaining a fragility and dependence that disarmed me entirely. In the time to come Sapna grew gradually more assured around the house, around me. Yet in the first months especially, when I came upon her doing something unusual, laughing at a joke Riz made, chatting too long with the milk-delivery boy, dusting her face in cheap foundation to look fairer, I could feel within this small rush of irritation, as if the gentle erosion of her dependence made me somehow less.

Every year the temperatures rose and the water problem worsened. Our fifth summer in the East End – Leila closing on three – the air was so dry you could hardly sweat. The newspapers led with panicked articles about the record-breaking heatwave. Snot clung to the wings of my nose and was painful to pinch out, breaking free in lumps like little stones. Leila began to get dizzy spells. She seemed tired all the time, pale. Her doctor said it was sun exhaustion. We had to be careful, make sure she got lots of water. We all felt it, an intense warmth like an infection, heat and anger rising inside you hand-in-hand, at street markets, trade grounds, sweet shops, liquor stores, anywhere people were forced to be outside, irruptions of white-hot rage. I suffered too. Sometimes Sapna would get it, sometimes one of the other servants. You couldn't help but explode.

The taps worked in spurts. Two hours in the morning, two at night, if you could call that water. They sputtered brown spots around the sink, leaving it like the toilet bowl at a highway stop. If the stream ever spiralled up to full strength it was half-clear and half-gravel-brown. The water scalded. Riz would joke to his friends that the bidet showers we'd installed were the first things to become useless. I bought extra plastic buckets and the servants filled them every morning, five or six in each bathroom, so the water could cool before we used it. Our society paid a bribe each month for even this limited supply. Every home had to contribute. We had to or we'd get nothing.

One afternoon that summer I'd taken a few minutes for myself. Riz was with buyers. I'd just come back from Leila's preschool. My head was throbbing. I asked for a nimbu pani, stretching out with a sudoku on the planter's chair in the living room, my feet up, the glazed picture window gelding the dark orange orb creeping west. When we moved here the trees from the park were all we could see but it was as if green had been drained from our view. Everything looked brown and yellow, lamps, parked cars, electricity poles, the road itself coated in fine dust.

It was hotter that summer than it'd been for a hundred years. Why do they tell us things like this? Trees sagged like broken men. Still no one followed the rules: the construction boom and the factories took the groundwater almost to zero. On TV they'd show clips of wailing Slum women, banging brass pots, dragging reporters by the wrist to the insides of dark huts. Children leaned dazed against the walls, their lips near transparent in the glare of the camera LED. They breathed in jerky, rapid gulps and cried without tears. A thin, dry smack after every word they could push out. The old folk looked even stranger, so pale they were tinged blue. The young men interviewed didn't talk to the reporter. Instead they shouted directly at the camera. Eyes flashing, cracked lips, chests out, they stared through the screen right at you and spat their words with choked anger, asking why their families had been ignored so long.

Doorbell. The maid's naked feet made ringing slaps on the marble. I slipped my legs off the long arms of the planter's chair. Naz was wearing jeans and a pink T-shirt, polo player and horse huge on one sleeve. He looked even more like a small weightlifter, chest straining against his shirt, the seam of each sleeve fitted around brick-like biceps.

'Get this place soundproofed,' Naz said. 'Then you won't have that racket.' This was typical. I hadn't seen him for months but he walked in gently chiding me as if we regularly exchanged homemaking tips.

'Hi Naz,' I said. 'How are you?'

'How can you sit like this?' He collapsed into a sofa just behind me. 'It's impossible.'

'Better than having the generator off.' That was the other big problem. The voltage had dipped so low you needed to run the generator to get the air conditioning working. We spent a shocking amount on diesel every month.

'Where is it, out in the balcony?'

'Yeah.'

'Build a shed. We've soundproofed our bedroom and the living room. A shed will keep out some of the noise.'

'Did you come to talk about the generator, Naz? Riz isn't home. He's taken some of his buyers out. What can I get you? Nimbu pani? You want a beer?'

'A beer? It's three in the afternoon, Shalini. You want to start drinking?' He made an exclamation that sounded like spitting. I turned in surprise. He was staring out of the window with a wrinkled expression.

'I'm not having one, Naz. I was offering you.'

He slapped his stomach hard, bouncing his palm off muscle. 'Haven't had a drink in eight months,' he said. 'I don't any more. Not since marriage. I go to the mosque every day now. Abbu-Ammi are very happy.'

'Really? That's new.'

'This city is falling apart, Shalini. It's dangerous. We need to stick together. Pray. All of us. You have to make sure Leila has the right education in these matters. There are schools where she can learn.'

'Riz and I haven't decided about that. Schools and so on.'

'I'm just saying, it's important. When I have kids . . .' He trailed off, staring absently now, out the tall windows. A skein of geese beat through the starch-blue expanse, headed in echelon to the hills just north, then unaided, over the great range, to the knot of sierras that make the roof of the world. 'It's too bad I missed Riz. I want you to give him a message.'

'What's that?'

'Abbu is unwell.' A wave of dismissal at my worried look. 'No, not yet. He's tough. He wants to sort things out before he gets sicker. That's why he sent me here. He wanted me to tell Riz he will get his fair share. Despite how things have been—' He broke off, searching for words. 'You know I like you, Shalini. Even in school I liked you. But there's no denying what you've done to our family.'

'Naz! How can you say that?'

'Riz left us. His family. Community. He left all that behind for you. I have to take care of our parents . . .' His Adam's apple popped out. 'Khair. That's not what I came to talk about.'

'No?'

'They're old people, Shalini. They're worried. What will happen to Leila? We are a society that needs order. Rules. We don't want her mixing with everyone.'

He looked so smug, lecturing me with his hands hooked behind the back of the leather couch, chest bulging like the breasts of women you see in the Olympics, wrestlers or shot-putters. Riz would be hopping mad if he were here. I was very angry myself. But I knew better than to get between the brothers. 'I don't think it's your job to tell us how to raise our daughter, Naz.'

'I care for her, Shalini. I care for my brother.'

'She has the best of everything. Look, no disrespect to Gazala. Your wife is beautiful. But I don't want my daughter in a burqa. No one cares about these things here. There are lovely parks. We're thinking of getting her admission in Yellowstone. You remember the fun we had there.'

'So you're going to send her to Yellowstone. There's a reason they don't have schools like that any more, Shalini. What-all they teach there. No values, no respect for elders, no respect for our past.' He stood and began walking up and down a patch of parquetry. Each step scuffed the rich polish. 'She'll grow up with no culture. Running around with boys from here and there. No sense of community. Is that what you want?'

'Nonsense. Is this the only idea of community we have? Riz and I don't want to live like that, Naz. That's why we found this place.'

'Nothing is easy, but there has to be some compromise, especially if you want Abbu to remember you when he goes. She's his only granddaughter. He hardly sees her.'

'You know how hard it is to come over? Even with our paperwork in order. Just because I wasn't born there. I keep telling them to come here, people can come and go as they please. But Abbu-Ammi won't set foot inside the East End.'

The maid walked in with a cup of tea and jam biscuits on a quarter plate. One of the servants had to run down to the mini-mart to get sugar, she explained, that was why it'd taken so long. Naz nodded at the table at his side and turned back to me without taking a sip.

'Where is Leila, actually? Bring her here. I have a gift in the car.'

'She's in her room. I've just brought her back from school.' I shouted for Sapna. There was no response so I rose, glad to be out of my brother-in-law's presence for even a few seconds. Leila's room was cool and dark and densely quiet. Empty. When I returned to the living room Naz was sprawled, a pink smear against the white leather couch. 'The maid must've taken her to the park,' I said.

Naz let out a loud snort.

'Something you wanted to say?' I asked.

For a few seconds he stared at me, running the tips of his fingers through the outcrop of hair at his chin. 'Say what you want about Gazala,' he said, standing up. He made for the door, then turned around. 'She might not know as much about the world as you. But she knows our culture. She wouldn't offer a guest a beer. Three in the afternoon! And if we had a little girl, at least Gazala would know where she was.'

I felt colour climb to my face, but the spurt of anger was quickly exhumed, replaced by a sense of shame, as if a wet, hot towel had been settled around my shoulders and face. As Naz neared the door I shouted, wretchedly, 'Wait. You've come all the way. Let's go to the park and find her. She'll be happy to see her Chachoo.'

Outside was pure white heat. The trees lolled towards us from either side of the road, bent by thirst. 'Sapna is so stupid sometimes,' I said. 'Why would she bring her out in this heat?'

'What time does Leila usually go out?'

'Five, sometimes six. I don't know what happened today. Unless Sapna is trying to meet that boyfriend of hers. She sneaks away sometimes so she can meet this guy.'

'Her boyfriend?' He let out a short laugh. 'Your maid has a boyfriend? Just what-all goes on in the East End? Bloody free-for-all.'

I nodded in agreement. 'It's too much. All these movies. Spends half her time getting ready. I don't know who she thinks is looking.'

The road was so hot my feet were soon like flat pans of fire, I should've worn shoes, not these thin sandals, and my hair like strands of burning rope. By the time we reached the quadrangle of green with the yellow, spoked fence both of us were silenced by the thick, stagnant air. Two teenage girls were on their knees, painting the inside walls and concrete benches of a small pavilion by the gate. We hurried to it. The trees gave little shade, the dark pavilion was a chance to cool our feet. Tins of paint were all about, a couple of spray cans strewn. The girls had used a stencil to make a large mural of the earth. The taller one had sprayed blue in elegant twirls, marking the currents in the ocean. Then she stepped away and the other, with cans of brown and green, had filled in the land masses. Once they were done with that they had begun to paint a series of round-headed stick figures on the earth's rim. The stick figures were joined to one another by their outstretched arms, a world of people holding hands. I tapped Naz and whispered, 'Can't you see why we're happy here? This is how Leila will grow up.'

He stared for a few seconds with a sullen smile. When he turned to me, one side of his face was screwed up as if squinting from the sun. 'Good idea,' he muttered. 'She'll be like you. Clueless about how the world really works.'

The park looked at first to be empty, but at the far end, just beneath the tree house, Leila and the maid were chasing each other around the dead stump of a tree. We left the pavilion, avoiding the heated concrete path by walking on the cracked soil. A spicy smoke tickled my nostrils like a sneeze. We hurried on.

Leila was wearing a pink sleeveless top that matched her hairband and knee-length shorts with a thick band of scrunched denim at the waist, little canines sticking out proudly. Her face and neck shone from an even layer of sweat. Sapna was dodging her, floating her dupatta in the breeze as a matador uses his cape, drawing Leila closer each time. As Leila would make her final lunge she'd let out a little squeal of pleasure, convinced she finally had her quarry. A brief wave of disappointment. Then she'd beetle after Sapna again, back straight, head down, tiny arms and legs frenetically pumping, determined.

I had a sense that Sapna noticed us but was pretending she didn't. I called out to my daughter a touch angrily. She swivelled in surprise and shouted 'Mummy' and came charging and wrapped her arms around my knees, knocking me off balance, making me laugh. Naz steadied us with a hand on my shoulder.

'I've brought you a present, little darling,' he said to her.

'Chachoo!'

'Did you just notice him?' I asked.

'I didn't see!' she laughed, panting heavily. 'What did you bring for me, Chachoo?'

'It's a surprise,' he said and knelt for a hug. 'But I left it in my car. When we go home I'll give it to you.'

My daughter jumped into his arms. Sapna was staring at Naz, her lips parted, twisting the end of her dupatta into a tiny knot. Another surge of annoyance. 'Why did you bring my daughter out in this heat?' I asked. 'You know she's not supposed to be in the sun.'

'She wasn't taking her nap. Wouldn't go to sleep.' Sapna bowed her head, letting out a small giggle. 'I thought we could play.'

'From now on you check with me, understand? Why do you think I'm there? I don't want you doing anything like this without my permission.'

'But I didn't do . . .' she began to complain, but checked herself. One thing I cannot abide is back talk in front of a guest. 'Okay, didi. I will ask.'

Naz and Leila were tossing about a slim blue disc with a perforated centre. The disc was meant to be thrown flat like a frisbee but Leila could not manage that so she and Naz were hurling it underarm at each other as if it were a shoe. Suddenly Naz halted the game, holding a hand up. A commotion of some sort was rising up the road. I walked the few steps to a mud gutter adjoining the park wall and spotted, through the yellow spokes, a group of chanting, marching men. There must've been forty or more, dressed in white shirts and trousers with black leather belts and shoes, striding in three rough columns. They carried long bamboo staves that they clattered against the street, giving resonance to their chants.

'Oh yes, the Repeaters have uniforms now.' Naz was by my side.

'Is that what this is?' I asked.

'Seems like it. They look quite smart actually.'

'I've never seen this before. Not here, I mean. Just look at them. They're always so angry.'

The Repeaters reached the park. Most had their backs to us. They'd been shouting a slogan all the way down the road. 'Unity! Purity! Unity from purity!' Now they were quiet, standing in a semi-circle, leaning heavily on the sticks they carried, mopping their foreheads with folded handkerchiefs, against their clothes, leaving grey-brown smears on the sleeves of their new shirts. One man strode to the front so everyone faced him.

'Holy shit! I know that guy,' Naz said.

'Which one?' I asked. It made me nervous to see these people so close to my home. I motioned silently for Leila to join me. She was standing with Sapna, watching.

'He's so much older now.'

'Who is?'

'That main guy. Their leader. He doesn't henna his moustache any more, he dyes it.' He was a broad, tall man, middle-aged, his hair slicked back and carefully dyed to leave a single spurt of white hair by his forehead. 'I'd recognise that clump of white hair anywhere. Look how far he's come. He used to be a Repeater at your sector's gates. Once he almost caught Riz and me trying to sneak in.' Naz joined the tip of his thumb to his index finger and held them up, grinning at the memory. 'This close. He came this close to catching us.'

The leader began to smash his stave against the road. The men started to scream. 'Come out, come out. Foreigner's tout. Traitors! Traitors!' It became clear that this mob had grouped at a specific point, a wicket gate hardly broader than a man, opening into a brick path lined with bushes. The path led to a small glass door, tinted brown, with posters on the front. The mob continued to chant, waving the Council's flag. Some could hardly contain their excitement, cracking their sticks on the ground, rocking a car parked by the side of the road. No surprise a few seconds later when we heard the brief soft crunch of a windshield splintering. I moved Leila so she was pressed between me and the park wall, and just then I saw, from the corner of my eye, a twitch of the curtains on the upper floor.

Shattering the windscreen had charged the men's blood. Now no pretence of military order. They milled about the gate with furious, frustrated steps, unsure what to do next, seething and sweating. Their leader shrugged and flung his free arm about, barking into a cell phone. The men at his side strained to hear the other end of the conversation. Three men hunted along the road for missiles. Soon they were gingerly passing from palm to palm rocks gathered from the earth. They lobbed these at the house. The stones smashed against the facade, showering plaster, cracked the lintel of a ground-floor window, landing with a thud on the lawn. One stone sailed against the dazzling afternoon sky in a high, pretty parabola, arcing through an upper bay window with a near-deferential tinkle, bringing down a curtain. Still you couldn't see inside because of the reflections of the trees in what remained of the glass. A lusty cheer went up. Then the chant started again. 'Traitors! Traitors!'

'Should we get out of here?' I whispered to Naz.

'I want to see. Don't worry. They're not bothered about us.'

A pack of mongrels that'd been barking at the mob sprinted off down the road and returned now, worrying at the tyres and magnet-grey doors of a sedan steered by a driver in a peaked cap and uniform and bearing at the back a couple reading newspapers. The mob swarmed the car as if it were carrion. One man swung his lathi onto the bonnet, setting the metal ringing, at which the woman clutched her husband's shoulder. But the leader of the mob leaned back and let out a roar. Immediately everyone backed off. The sedan wriggled out and away like a fish from a net.

The house door opened with a squeal of rust. For some seconds there was silence; you could hear the birds that hadn't yet escaped the deep summer. A little man, so dark the rims of his eyeballs looked jaundiced, with bouncing, neck-length curls. He was wearing an office peon's brown shirt and pants. As soon as he stuck his head out that vigorous lust-filled scream started up again. The peon shrank back into the house as if guided by some primordial instinct, smooth as a snail's feelers, and seeing this the leader of the mob laughed out loud. Everyone quickly joined in. As the rest continued to laugh, without saying a word, the leader began twirling his staff around his head, like a wrestler with an Indian club. This was a signal. Whipping through the air with gathering speed, spittled frenzy lathering his face, hysteria riding in circles around the surrounding mob. A flash from a childhood television show with chariots and gold paper crowns: 'Aakraman!' But there was no call to attack. Instead the men simmered around the gate.

When the peon emerged again he was bundled out onto the path. He took a few heavy steps to steady himself. Halfway down the mud track now, he hunkered his shoulders in entreaty, hands joined in front of his face, terror in his yellow eyes, in his crooked knees, in the unheard babble incessant on his lips. When he found his voice it quivered with each word.

'Sirs, sirs, please,' he said. 'Madam-Sir are not here. They aren't in town.'

'Don't lie to us!' someone shouted. 'We know they are.'

'Please believe. They're not here, I'm telling you. They have gone fact-finding. To the mines.'

Naz's stare flitted between the leader and the peon, his lips tightly pressed. 'Let's get out of here, Naseer,' I whispered. 'We can take the other gate. I want to get Leila home.'

'Two minutes, two minutes,' Naz said.

The leader of the Repeaters walked to the front of the group, sharpening his collar fold as he moved. 'What's your name?'

'Mohan, sir. Mohan.'

'Where are you from?'

'From the mines, only, sir. I used to work there. Madam-Sir gave me a job in the city.'

The Repeater had walked right up to the gate. 'Come out. We won't hurt you.' The peon turned for a long look at the house, perhaps at the upper windows. Did I see a shadow flit across the glass or was that a reflection, a bird or a movement in the tree? He walked slowly towards the gate.

'Are you married?' asked the Repeater, adopting a friendlier tone as the man approached.

'No, sir. I am working only.'

'Do they make you work very hard?'

'Sometimes, sir. City life is tough. I did not know about these walls.' He pulled the gate open and gingerly stepped out onto the road. 'They all look the same. I keep getting lost.'

Repeater and peon faced each other, the latter dark and small, arms held together in silent imploration. The Repeater turned to his flock. 'Did you hear that, men? The little fellow is confused by the walls. He doesn't understand the city.' At this everyone began to laugh.

An uncertain smile appeared on the peon's face. The two were now alongside, facing the crowd, less than a lathi's length between their shoulders. Suddenly a muscled arm snaked out, the Repeater taking hold of the peon's collar and twisting him onto his toes. As if he weighed nothing he hurled the yelping man onto the road. 'Do you know what your Sir-Madam are doing?' he shouted, spit flying like silver bullets in the sunlight. 'They are traitors. Stopping the work that will make this city rich, make us strong, using foreign money. Traitors!'

Maybe the peon expected this. No sooner had he hit the road than he bounced back around and dived at the leader's feet. I covered Leila's eyes and ears. He had his hands folded again and was tapping the Repeater's shoes, saying, 'Please sir, let me go, I'm a poor man, I don't know anything.' I could no longer see him. The squad had closed in. One man raised a staff to the air. It came whistling down and I heard an anguished scream. 'Tell us where they are,' someone screamed. 'Are they inside? Are they inside?' A rain of lathis. The leader had taken a few steps back and watched with a smug smile.

I elbowed Naz. 'This is making me sick. I'm going. You come when you want.'

'You sure? It might not be safe . . . you can't wait?'

'I'm sure. Why do you have to watch this?'

'Are they inside?' someone called.

'Where are they then?'

'They must be here!' the shouting continued.

'I want to see what happens,' Naz said. I grabbed Leila's hand and we hurried to the other end of the park. Sapna picked up the toys and followed. As we approached the rear gate, amid the shrieks, the insults, the whistling lathis and the yelps, the peon could be heard, in a drawn-out, hiccupping sob that barely reached us, 'Upstairs. Upstairs. They are both upstairs.'

II

The morning we found out about Leila's school admission was so hot the sun powering through the windows bounced off the mirror face of a juice decanter and turned a newspaper left in the breakfast nook to kindling. Stupidity, self-involvement prevented me from seeing this for what it was. A portent. The three of us could have run to the end of the earth. Yet I thought nothing of it. We managed to get the smoke out of the curtains. But Leila had a bad stomach, the heat had got to her. I had to go that day. There was all this paperwork only I could make sense of. I insisted we couldn't leave Leila with the ayah. Riz made a few calls and announced that he would work from home. I decided to take Sapna with me; if they needed even more photocopies, notifications for notaries, what have you, she could run down to the shop in the small market by the school.

It wasn't a long drive to Yellowstone. Driving up, I looked for the last time upon those famous spires, the clock tower, the four maroon pillars extending past the second floor to the portico's triangular hat. The jhoolabaadi was empty, as was the river of sparkling Bermuda grass, sprinklers dancing everywhere. What a luxury, in this grimmest summer, to have these fripp-frippering jets of crystal water running their circuit. It couldn't last. Yellowstone was gutted in the weeks to come, as the mobs began to hunt for difference.

When Riz and I were students the best schools were independent, but by the time Leila had reached the right age almost every school in the city was affiliated with a particular sector. The richer communities had acquired the better schools and put them behind one set of walls or the other. Yellowstone, the oldest and best, was the final holdout, the last mixed school in the city.

I was nervous about Leila's admission. It's been sixteen years but I remember so many things. Waiting at the gate with the other parents. Calling to tell Riz the news as I walked to my car, stilettos crunching into the gravel.

Both of us laughing, crying, proud of our daughter, she'd impressed them all, though sweat streams ran down my back and the parking lot soil had kicked up into dust devils and the wind was like the blast behind a window AC. I hurried to the car, where Sapna fanned herself with one of my glossies. The smell of her sweat filled my car. Even Sapna was happy, when I told her, raising a hand to her mouth to hide her nervous smile, nodding with wonder at the sprawling school.

It struck noon just as we made it to the traffic light at the end of the road. The dashboard display read high-fifties. Along the road, about halfway up the wall, a digital hoarding showed CGI images of a new residential complex inside the sector for Kamrupi Brahmins, completion date undetermined. Couples walking with prams along glittering emerald lawns. Indoor and outdoor pools. Private temple, fully modernised. Driving range simulators for golfers. Twenty-four-hour power backup, twenty-four-hour water. My eye was drawn to a movement underneath the hoarding, a glint of yellow blurred by the heat shimmers in the air. A man in a lemon kurta-pyjama was getting to his feet. Strange, because the beggars knew better than to walk around at this time of the day. He was staring at me. As soon as I met his gaze I knew it was a mistake. Without waiting even for a change in the lights he walked calmly through the lanes of barrelling traffic, directly towards our car. Both sides of the road tyres began to squeal. One driver got out of his car – a chain of screeching brakes – and produced a thick ribbon of abuse before hurtling away. The old man was far from calm, this was clear as he got closer, his shoulders jerking up and around, his head shaking like a paint mixer.

'What a strange man,' I said to Sapna. 'I wonder what he's doing.'

'He's looking right at us, didi.'

He'd crossed the last lane. He was nearing the traffic light. We couldn't move – cars, two-wheelers hemmed us in from every angle. I checked the central locking. This man negotiated the stream of cyclists and then took position, arms by his side, underneath the digital display reporting in red numerals how many seconds you have until the light changes. No one around us seemed aware of his presence. When he reached us he planted himself on the bonnet, knees on the bumper, staring into my eyes. A monk's fringe of white hair above his ears. Sapna screamed and grabbed the door handle uselessly. The car keened forward with his weight. I couldn't move. He was chanting to himself, praying perhaps. Sweat around his undershirt had left a thick horseshoe. Sapna was pulling at my left sleeve. I made to clamp down on the horn, but as soon as he saw me move he threw himself back and scurried away. My hand hit the horn anyway, producing a bitty little beep. The forlorn honk – or perhaps relief – made us both laugh.

In a minute he was in front of us again, down on his haunches, his back against the rear door of the white car in front of me. The car had a woman and a driver. The woman stared at her phone, oblivious. The old man jumped upright with surprising speed, jerked back his head and stared directly at the sky, as if drawing strength from it. He flung open the door and pulled the woman out by her wrist in one smooth motion. She came out dangling like a child's stuffed toy, her face flashing by us – cheeks sucked in, eyebrows wide apart, the casual safety of the previous moment now unbearably distant. I hit my horn, she screamed, the driver leapt from the car all at the same time. The old man paid none of this any attention. He dragged her to the front. Flung her to one side with a roll of his arm so she slumped onto the bonnet of the car. As quickly, he jumped into the back seat and locked all the doors.

The woman sobbed by the side of the road. People shouted at the driver for leaving the key in the ignition, the engine running. The old man was going nowhere. He had his neck up so his throat was directly in front of the air-conditioning vents. He yanked at his kurta collar and let air down his front. He began swaying his head back and forth in excitement until he was landing with such force onto the back seat that the car began to rock. This went on. Then a driver from another car figured out a way to open the lock on the driver-side door. Each time he got it open the old man flicked it shut with a cheeky grin. The woman was still sobbing. The car horns did not ease up once in these minutes, merging into one, a tilting groan. Eventually a bunch of drivers distracted the old man by pretending to open both front doors at once. He dug in with all his strength, his buttocks as anchors and arms as struts, pushing against the roof. It took four men. They pulled him out by his legs. One man slapped him half-heartedly. We all saw the old man was not quite a beggar, that he'd been driven mad by this violet heat. We left him sitting on the concrete divider of the road, his yellow kurta spread around him, head rocking, fingers gripping the back of his neck.

When we were moving again it was hard to grip the wheel. My fingers were trembling. 'That was too much, Sapna. Too much.'

'Very scary, didi.'

'It looked so easy. He pulled her out of the car in just a second.'

She didn't say anything. After a few moments I muttered, 'We don't mind, you know . . .'

'Yes, didi?'

'If someone comes to me for money, you know I always give. You've seen. I always give.'

I felt deflated. My head ached. The sun bouncing off the roads and windshields. We drove in silence. In the past months the unrelenting heat had widened the cracks, all over the city the roads coming apart like the gaps in an old person's mouth. We turned onto the long arterial avenue that leads to the East End.

Immediately we were surrounded by cars. More traffic. The pressure at my temples had been climbing. Now I felt fit to blow. We were so close to home that my toes curled with frustration, I wanted to slam on the accelerator and plough my way through. On my left a bus had come in at an angle, attempting to sneak into my lane. Tired, dirty faces peered down greedily. The divider was to my right, its black stripes like mirrors in the sun, with a long trough of earth so dry it was cracked into bolts of lightning. An optimistic soul had jammed dozens of mesh cylinders into the soil. Nothing grew.

'What is this now?' I asked.

'I know,' Sapna said, staring at the massive red cloth hovering in the air in the distance. It rested on bamboo poles. Silver horns were lashed down where one pole met the other. The batik awning waved prettily in a breeze, though around us the air seemed perfectly still. 'It's a political rally,' Sapna continued, smiling. 'Look, didi, Ashish should also be here. Even the people from my basti are here. They've come about the water problem.' She shrugged towards a stream of women and men who sat in the dirt beyond the footpath. The line of people travelled to the awning, stopping at a bamboo barrier. Each had a metal pot beside them. The women shaded their faces with their saris. Some men had tied handkerchiefs around their heads. There were children too, lying flat on their backs, ministered by their mothers. The aluminium pots glinted like diamonds.

'Ashish? Who is Ashish?'

'Ashish is my man, didi. So many times I've told you.'

Ludicrous that they're allowed to block the road like this, the main road leading to the East End. I exchanged an exasperated smile with the woman in the car that the bus had tried to overtake. Soon enough, liveried drivers emerged from the Mercs and Beemers, gathering into a group and moving towards the tent, shining metal on their peaked caps.

'Yes, yes, of course.' I did remember. He waited outside the East End gates for Sapna most evenings. Dark fellow with a mullet of sorts, always running his fingers through a crimped, throat-length beard. 'But why is he here?'

'He works with Joshijee. Three years he has worked

with him, since the water went. Joshijee has promised to get water to our basti again.'

'Three years? You haven't had water for three years?' I tried to keep scepticism from my voice. They tend to magnify their woes, hoping for sympathy, some kind of payout.

'Yes, didi. We used to have four handpumps for the basti. One handpump stopped working, then another. It's become really bad. For three years, nothing.'

'How do you live?'

'We survive. I'm one of the lucky ones. By your kindness I use the servant bathroom.'

A low murmur filtering into my awareness. A chant coming from the people queued up along the side of the road. It had started from the front of the line, like current moving down a circuit. The men and women next to us joined in. A song, with verses of kinetic call-and-response. I braved the slap of heat, sliding down the window.

'*Yeh azaadi jhooti hain*,' the front of the line screamed.

'*Jhooti hain, jhooti hain*,' shouted the rest.

'*Yeh azaadi jhooti hain*,' they screamed.

'*Jhooti hain, jhooti hain*.'

'What a strange song,' I said, rolling up the window. 'What do they mean, freedom is a lie?'

'It's water, didi. It's driven everyone mad. These are the people from my basti only. Joshijee told Ashish to bring them.'

'This Joshi, he is the one on TV all the time?'

'Yes, didi. He comes on the news, no?' she said. Doubt crept into her voice. 'Their leader? I'm not sure. Ashish works for him. He helps him with everything he needs.'

'Your boyfriend works with the Council?'

'No, no, Ashish is like me, he's also from the Slum, not educated like you all. He works for Joshijee. His helper. As Joshijee has become more important, Ashish's responsibilities have grown.' She smiled proudly. 'Now he takes care of many things.'

'You're going to marry him?'

'Ashish says this is not the time, didi. Joshijee has a few things planned for the summer. Once those are over we can get married.'

In a red hatchback a few feet away a young couple was rolling a joint. The boy was arranging the constituents on his palm as she rooted around in the back seat. A purple spaghetti strap travelled over a circular tattoo on her left shoulder.

'What do you do for water?'

'Tankers come.'

'Every day? How can you afford it? Even I can't afford it every day.'

'We share the tanker between all of us, didi. Each person gets two buckets. It's never enough. People are late to work because the lines are so long. They lose their jobs. Some women, the old ones, they get into fights.' A patch of sweat that grew like a brinjal at her armpit had been dried by the AC, though the discoloration remained. 'Ashish was the first one to take on the tanker mafia. I told him not to. He didn't listen.'

'What did he do?' I asked.

'Actually, didi,' she looked at the cars surrounding us, 'do you mind if I go there for five minutes? I don't think anyone will be able to move for some time. I would love to see Ashish on stage. With such big people. Joshijee, the Council. All the important sector people.'

In the years since our wedding I'd felt a rising irritation in myself when there was any talk of the Council, purity, the segmentation they were determined upon. Usually I wanted to shut it out. But today I wanted to see this Joshi who sent out his gangs of toughs, producing these surgical vibrations of violence.

'Okay, we'll go. But wait.' The sky was hospital blue, a clear border at one edge. The sun leered down. 'See if there's a dupatta in that tailor's bag.'

I wrapped the dupatta around my head and we stepped outside. The contrast with the AC was too much; within steps my head started to spin. I leaned against a vehicle. The heated metal singed my back. Sapna took my keys and ran to my car, returning with a thermos of water. The young couple in the hatchback stared at us blankly through a chamber of blue smoke. When I felt better, we walked across the nickering cars to the footpath, searching for shade. Some of the Slummers' metal pots had animal and plant motifs. The women shielded their faces from the glare and prying eyes. I drove on this road every day, but only now I noticed how these trees too were suffering. Insects had bored into the bark; branches were wilting or had fallen to the ground; the leaves scorched brown. The singing started up again, *'Yeh azaadi jhooti hain,'* like a backbeat to our steps. *'Jhooti hain, jhooti hain.'* Denim clung slimily to my legs. The last few steps I could feel my head turning light again, and I had to stop at a giant floor fan, its thick draught flailing my curls, the sweat off my body.

The stage had a fluttering, shiny-white backdrop. There was a solitary microphone at the front, behind it seated rows of older men, some in formal suits, a couple of priests, imams, bishops in clashing vestments. Elders from the high sectors, representing the important communities.

Under the awning the audience was divided into numerous zones, a rope running between them at waist height. Chairs had been placed for the people from the highest sectors. Olive army-surplus mattresses laid out for the middle communities. The section we had reached, for the Slummers, wasn't actually under the awning. We sat in the sun, floor fans turned in our direction.

There must've been three thousand around me. As Sapna led me through the rows of squatting people my eyes began to drip from the ammoniac stench of stale clothes, collective sweat. Grumbles as we bumped against knees and shoulders. A group of older women said something about my jeans. My bracelet, my earrings. I could feel their eyes.

Finally, Sapna found an unoccupied spot. 'Look,' she whispered, as we sat down. She was gleaming now, leaning forward, her fingers undoing and redoing the top button of her kurta. Her boyfriend was bent at the waist, walking amid the seated men on stage, his beard flickering as the currents from the huge fans clashed. Whenever anyone whispered something he nodded vigorously and did a small salute. A shiny green suit in the first row wiggled his fingers at him. Ashish took the microphone, adjusted its height, tapped on it a few times. 'Chyek', he said, and disappeared backstage.

In the hiatus a stupor settled. A few rows down an old man with a neck like snakeskin shook himself awake. The woman next to me hitched her sari up and began to scratch an old mosquito bite just underneath where the bone protrudes at the ankle. She stared at me with unabashed interest as she used a fingernail to pick at it. The wound, a small black ring with a flaky white centre, looked deeply ugly against her dark skin. A spot of scarlet appeared and bubbled into a small drop. This she wiped with the pulp of her grubby finger. I turned away, suddenly sick, desperate to move to the better section, where at least the men weren't all wearing this stinking polyester.

In the front, beyond the people seated on the mattresses, each person had their own metal folding chair. The women wore fashionable saris, some blouses cut low at the back. Beads of sweat ran down the neck of a woman perched upon a chair in the last row of that section, streaking the cake of white powder along her spine. A small, yellowish man with an incipient paunch walked on stage. The audience under the awning was in thrall, their applause thundered as Joshi approached the mic. He gave that speech hundreds of times that summer. Even now they show it on television all the time.

'My friends,' Joshi said – this also producing a long round of claps – 'we have started to climb the long ladder. We will scale the mountain once again. And, let me tell you, we are very close now' – a finger climbing into the air – 'close to making our land pure, ourselves pure, pure as the land of the ancients. Soon we will be mentally, emotionally, culturally restored. Soon we will reclaim our rightful place at the top of the world.'

He paused and looked around. 'We must live according to our own great principles. Our history. Why must we live with compromise? Our purity has been perverted over the centuries. Centuries of rule by outsiders have led to spiritual subjugation. But the atrocities of this age can be combatted. They are nothing but a passing phase. Our cultural roots are too firm, struck deeply into the spring of immortality. We will once again find that purity, the purity that comes from order, from respect, from each of us remembering our communities. Our roles. What runs in our blood.'

'My friends, turn to the right, I want you all to turn to the right. Look where the unfortunate souls sit.' He raised his arm in a high semi-circle until it landed on the section Sapna and I were in. 'These people are not from any sector. They are from the Slum. I want you to think. There is a young boy who works for me. His name is Ashish.' A squeal, quickly stifled, Sapna's eyes shining. 'Ashish might be born outside the sectors, but he has proved himself capable in his years of service. He tells me the water supply has stopped to his home. To all their homes. Looking at these people today, does your heart not break? I feel so much sorrow. We must help them also. We must make sure they are not left behind.'

Another round of ovation from the front sections, those seated on chairs. Smattered applause in the middle segment. In our section there was silence. One man, a few rows behind me, shouted loudly, 'How? How will you help?' But Joshi seemed not to hear him.

'Soon we will get to the unfortunates, but first we must complete our work!' he shouted, arms raised in a V. 'Still there are places in the city where boundaries are not respected. Can we be a true society if some do not observe our rules? There are people in this city who seem to crave disorder. The people who have ruled you for so long. Politicians, judges, bureaucrats, media. They work together, all of them. They have made us impure with their impure rule. No respect for our oldest rules. This is why I've called you here, to this spot. Do you know who lives in the sector behind me? Do you know what they call this – the East End? They think they're better than us. They think they know better than our respected ancestors. They think they know better than the rules that governed us for centuries.'

I was shocked. Sapna bowed her head, quiet. I felt nauseous, my head spinning. Pins, needles spread to elbows and forearms and then down to my fingers. Why did these people care how we lived?

'This is not our culture,' Joshi continued. 'Our heritage. I have promised you the perfect home. A place of order, discipline, clean and pure. Those who do not obey our rules must feel the strength of our history.'

The elders rose as one, the orange-robed priests, the dumpy imams, the thin bishop and his Protestant counterpart, and the rest, in suits and kurta-pyjamas, whose provenance I could not tell. They cheered with their hands above their heads. The Repeaters were here too, tucked away in a corner in their vestal white, making a ruckus, whooping, cracking their lathis against one another like swords, throwing them into the air. My head spun like a Newton disc, blurring into one thought, one colour.

'Give me a chance. I will make us pure,' Joshi shouted, voice stretched with lust. 'Each must protect our walls, our women, our communities. Make sure they cannot break our rules any more. Go forth and do our work. Once again we will reach the pinnacle of the world!'

I collapsed. The heat, fear, something else. My forehead slumped against the back of the person seated in front of me. Falling, I saw a dome of curved blue with a tiny white plane climbing to its centre, the perky angle of ascent making it seem proud, noble. I hit the ground and knew no more.

III

The bartender has a knowing smile above his bow tie. Am I drunk already? This will be my third flute. Time to slow down. A few feet from him, a huge fish carved from ice, a character from Leila's favourite movie, slowly drips from recognition. Pyramids of crystal-cut glasses have been arranged to face bottles of grenadine and tequila, champagne, vodka, gin and white wine. One side of the lawn is our small pool, lazurite from the tiles. Yelping infants and young mothers, the lucky ones back in their bikinis. Dark, slight, curly-haired nannies stand just outside the splash zone, preserving their best outfits, smiles and towels to the ready. Along the other side of the lawn an array of inflatable slides and bouncy castles, red and yellow vigorous in the 4 p.m. sun. Riz got permission from our neighbours so we could have the lawn to ourselves. He paid a preposterous bribe to the water officials so they would fill the pool. He wanted to show our friends we were happy, despite all that has been going on.

Riz comes up. 'You're fine, na? Don't dehydrate. It's only been two weeks. Remember what the doctor said.'

I take water from a tray that hovers by me. It's so hot we have a separate waiter wending his way between the guests with only water bottles. Since my episode at the rally I've been staying out of the sun. Riz squeezes my hand, picks up a beer, wanders into a conversation with two squash buddies. I watch from over my refilled glass. They're out on the lawn, standing by a serried rank of stone fish that arc water into a tiny moat. Riz is in his day-party-gear, linen shirt, this time pink stripes, grey shorts that show off his calves. As soon as he joins the conversation a woman I don't recognise appears at their side. She's in sunglasses and a summer dress that's all straps. She titters at something and puts her hand on Riz's forearm. A delicate flirtation, a weighted pause of her outspread fingers. I imagine Riz balling his fist so that his forearm is flexed. Then they're all laughing and I have a horrible feeling they've realised I'm watching.

'Bad form, Shal. You can't stare at your own husband,' Dipanita says, walking up behind me. She is in a thin white shirt that shows an orange bra, matched with white shorts from which her legs emerge in the shade of a new American penny.

'I was looking beyond him actually. To the food tents.' Three orange and red shamianas have been set up, under which men in white coats and chef hats make vegetarian and non-vegetarian pasta, hot dogs, burgers, various kinds of chaat and gol gappas. A DJ bounces in headphones, wiry assistant by his side, though there is no one yet on the wooden dance floor laid out to protect the grass.

'Yeah right. Who is that woman anyway?'

'It's good to see you, Dips. You're looking lovely.'

'I was so glad to hear Leila got in.'

'You didn't think of Yellowstone, did you? For your own kids?'

'Atul wouldn't. He couldn't imagine why we should. You know how stubborn he can be.' She puts one arm on her hip and pretends to push a pair of imaginary glasses up her nose, '"You want to send them out into that filth every day?"' She copies his nasal inflection so well it makes me giggle. '"When we have such good schools here? They'll be safe in our sector. No one will do anything, no danger."' We both laugh quietly. 'I don't know, Shal. Maybe he's right. Any other mother would think of safety first.'

'You mustn't let him say things like that to you.' At the other end of the party, one of our school friends, Nakul, is running his fingers through the inside of his empty mojito glass, pulling out the mint leaves and tossing them into his mouth. 'What about Pari and Anshu? How do they like it?'

'They seem fine. Didn't even notice. Atul is like his parents, of course. They all think it's a goddamn blessing. Come on, let's get a drink.'

'I need to take it easy. You get. I see the husband is looking for me again. Look at his face. He's annoyed about something.'

Riz waves at Dipanita, who returns a cheeky nod before slinking off. He comes to me smiling, but hisses into my ear, 'Did you invite Naz and Gazala? Why are they here?'

They are at the entrance, a few steps beyond the white wooden board with protruding metal hooks on which the valet drivers hang the keys of the cars they park, like that game you used to see in fetes and hill stations, a white-paper panel with neat rows of coloured balloons to fire an air rifle at. Gazala's slender frame is sheathed in a flowing single-pleat abaya, black with a grey satin strip running across her chest. She wears it with a dusty-pink silk hijab that brings out her alabaster complexion. Cheeks glowing with rouge. This is probably as much sun as she ever gets. Naz is like a lumpy action figure by her side, surveying the party, curling a lip when his eye rests on the men and women chatting in the pool. He nods at a few folk. In the crook of his arm is a small bike with pink training wheels and ribbons trailing from the handlebar.

'What was I supposed to do, Riz? Not call them? They're Leila's aunt and uncle. They know it's her birthday. They would've been so upset.'

'I don't give a shit! He's got a lot of fucking nerve, showing up after he spoke to you like that.'

'I'm not bothered, am I? It's in the past. Why are you getting het up?'

'Because he has no right to speak to my wife like that. Telling you these things. If he has a problem he better fucking come to me.'

'*Your* wife.' Now I was angry. 'It's your daughter's birthday. Put that male ego aside for once.'

'Why do you take his side? You're the one who was so angry . . . It's okay for him to tell you how to raise our daughter? To say all those things?'

'You know that's not what I meant. Just for Leila. Be the bigger brother.'

'I know why he's here. Because Abbu is unwell. He wants to sort out the property. That's all he gives a shit about. He calls me three times a week.'

The catering manager comes scurrying to us. I head to their tent to sort out an ice emergency. The sun has almost set, the sky lit up in yellow and saffron, tattered dabs of empty cloud, ventrals luminous gold, dorsals all muddy grey.

==

By dark everybody is more than drunk. The hooded underwater lights have turned the pool green. Lemon arabesques bob on its surface. Only a few people are in the water now, shoulders immersed to keep away a chill, pale faces spectral against the water. The wooden panels of the dance floor vibrate like guitar strings from the stomping feet. The DJ knocks a beat into the air. Clenched fist. Upright finger. Leila and her friends are upstairs, chlorine showered off and changed, animated movie on the big screen. They will drift to sleep one by one as the nannies gossip in the corner. I go up to make sure the mattresses have been laid out okay for the kids and the ayahs are given cake.

Heading downstairs, gradually aware that I haven't eaten anything myself, that an emptiness presses up against my insides. I steady myself for a few seconds against the thick teak bannister, sit heavily on the second step. It isn't that sickly, spinning drunk. I'm relieved, elated even. Everything has gone well. Now we will cut loose, there will be pink and blue shots and selfies and talk of how much life has changed in the ten years since school.

I look up, ready to re-enter the party, and Naz is standing in front of me. I first notice his thighs, like unripe, knobbly papayas. Overhead lights bounce off the marble, fill the air hard yellow.

'How're you feeling?' he asks.

'You're still here? After the lecture you gave me that day? Didn't think this was your scene.'

He scratches his beard noisily. 'Bhai is being a dick.'

'Where's Gazala?'

'Driver took her home.'

'Why would you do that?'

'I don't want her here. Not around this.' His chin draws up slightly, lips a slim, scarlet line. 'Why won't Riz take my calls? He blew me off when I went to talk to him. Acted like I wasn't there.'

'You should've known not to talk to me like that.' The alcohol has given me courage. 'We've dealt with this crap since we started dating. I don't need a lecture from you.'

'What lecture, man. I was only looking out for you guys.'

'I really thought you liked me, you know.' Trying my best not to slur, to leave my words undiminished. 'Then you repeat this bullshit that's going on outside. Come on, Naz.'

Eyes and mouth sag at either end, but there is something theatrical to his contrition. 'Will you talk to Riz for me?'

'He knows what he's doing. Why should I tell him what to do?'

A man and woman come lurching into the marbled foyer, holdings hands and laughing. One of Riz's buyers. When we were introduced a few hours earlier he said his wife was out of town. The tails of the shirt he's thrown over his swim trunks are soaked. They're looking for the stairs but stop short, still laughing, when they see us. Naz gives a disgusted look. The man bows, twirling his right hand, spins them both round and out into the night.

For some seconds there is only the pounding music. Finally, Naz says, 'Riz knows what he's doing, doesn't he?'

'What do you mean?'

'Just that. It's in his interest not to talk to me. In both your interests.'

When he flings his arms out, I burst out laughing.

'Great. Laugh, laugh. What do you think, I'll let you take it all?'

'Are you crazy, Naz? What's gotten into you?'

'I've figured it out. If Abbu dies, Riz will get everything. He's the older one. Then what splitting? He'll take the factory, all the land.'

'Is that what you think? We would do something like that?'

'I'm sorry, Shalini.' He pulls a phone from his pocket and punches in a number while walking to the doors leading to the lawn. I rest my back against the sharp edge of a step. Phone between shoulder and ear, he places a hand on a door handle, turns around and mutters from the side of his mouth, 'Leila deserves better. She should know her culture. Not grow up like this.'

Round about ten the music changes, stalking seamlessly from film-dance to something spikier, the beat faltering

– gauche – then swirling suddenly. Dipanita is on the grass without her shoes, giving off a gentle whiff of the poseur, only three buttons of her shirt still done up, eyes closed, palms pressed to her temples, feet kicking side to side in a whirring shuffle step, every fingerbreadth of coppery skin bursting with exothermic glow. The cups of her bra are like orange beacons under the scanners. Perhaps forty people left, between the dance floor and the grass, drinking around the narrow moat, the gurgling fish now lit up lichen green. Riz is alone on the small flight of steps between garden and house, surveying everything with a tranquil, cellophane aspect to his eyes that makes me think one of his friends brought dope.

I tell one of the waiters, a hair-gelled fellow with a flaking birthmark covering half a cheek, to fish the moulded-plastic champagne flutes and whisky cups out of the pool. That's when I hear shouting at the gate. The guard bleating some kind of refusal as a crowd of fervid, guttural voices encircle his pleas. Sharp anger. The old guard cries out loud. He is there to open the gates when we drive up, take packages from couriers, turn the generator on. Not this. Twelve, fifteen men bound in, swinging their lathis like golf clubs at my daisies and petunias and the low halogen lamps lining the pathway. It is immediately surreal, as if a scene from the Slum is being acted out for us. I feel sick, my stomach churns, all at once aware of the bitter spirits that slam against its walls. Everything keels, but then something within asserts itself: adrenal clarity, the world-at-drunk-speed fading away. The clomp of the Repeaters' boots, the shocked howls from my guests, the whip of lathis through the air, sometimes riffling the leaves, sometimes breaking the spines of the big bushes – all this happens in slow motion, as if home and garden and everyone in it is encased in amber. They go through the flower beds, toeing up clods of damp dirt, the white trousers and shirts I saw for the first time when they came for the couple who lived across the park. Riz is no longer near the stairs. He is nowhere to be seen. He's left? He wouldn't have. *How could he?* I'm sweating now, but shivering too.

DJ Gaurav only spots them when they have garrisoned the lawn. A Repeater climbs onto the low platform. Gaurav brings his hands together, eyes green from the lights. The Repeater uses the bottom of his staff to prod him in the chest. He raises the lathi over his head and comes down on the electrical equipment time and again, triangle sparks that fade to black. The dance lights go off, we are almost in darkness, only the few garden lamps that still stand are working.

Our friends are gathered in a tight knot, half on the dance floor, half off it. The men have formed a loose perimeter.

Some are shouting into their phones. Each face shows private panic. I am halfway to the bouncy slides, frozen, as the waiters and bartenders are shepherded to a food shamiana. A Repeater sticks his face into each of the serving trays, sniffing for contraband meats. When done he kicks the tray to the ground, senseless in his anger, his disgust.

Then there is my husband's voice, cracking slightly as he strains for volume, 'What the hell is going on here?'

Everyone turns. Riz stands at the top of the stairs with a brass candlestick and a child's cricket bat loosely gripped in either hand. I haven't a clue where he found them. The foyer lights make him glow. He drops the bat at his feet and brandishes his cell phone in the air. 'Any idea whose house you're in?' he shouts, his chest forward, legs shivering with rage. 'You know who I can call? Get out of here before I have you all thrown in jail.'

For a few seconds no one says anything. The hoodlums on the lawn look desperate to get to Riz, but something is holding each of them back, a thread hobbles them, mad horses spancelled by an invisible rein. 'But who will you call, Nawabzaada?' It is a taut voice, smooth as honey oak, ringing out behind me, slicing the young silence. The first thing I see is a dollop of white hair. 'Tell me now, who – who will you call?' Unmistakably, the same Repeater who led the charge the other day, walking with a deliberate tread down the garden path, an emperor entering a battlefield after the vanguard has supped.

Rizwan does not respond. He's racing through his phone book when a young Repeater hits him from behind, swinging a lathi with all his might onto Riz's lower back, sending him springing forward, the candlestick falling from his fingers, arched, head thrown back, a straitened cry escaping. He finds no footing and tumbles down the steps. Bizarrely, the leader of the Repeaters and I are running towards my husband at the same time, from opposing ends of the lawn. Nakul, one of our oldest friends, Riz's usual squash partner, is charging to the steps himself. Out of nowhere a lathi spins through the air and catches him just below the Adam's apple. He falls to the ground, unable to scream, whimpering and clutching his throat. His wife runs to him and she is yanked to a stop by her ponytail, collapsing to her knees.

Riz is breathing in quick gasps when I reach him. I cradle his head. Then I sense the arrival, tremors from the pounding feet, the stench of angry sweat, the drawled invective, it comes from all around, every point on the wheel, closer and still closer until we are subsumed, struck by knees and feet and fists, pushed down to the soil. When I blink out the blur from the tears I see the streaming gash above his eye, his shirt bloody and ripped to the waist. Our guests are in two lines, men and women. I have been separated from the group.

'What did you think?' the leader shouts. He is walking in between the two lines of guests, looking into the men's faces, appraising the women. 'Everywhere we are dying for water and you live like this? Rules don't apply to you? Giving bribes?'

A Repeater is standing behind me, a flabby man with a sharply sloping forehead. I turn and he raises his stick, bringing it down on my thigh. As I recoil my legs open and he slips the stick into the slit of my long dress. Suddenly the leopard-print triangle below my belly button is showing. 'This one is dressed like a hotel whore,' the Repeater says, laughing. I cover my thighs again but everyone has seen. The sense of unreality has not dimmed. I'm suddenly ashamed that I sprinkled my panties when I peed earlier.

'Bring her here,' the leader orders. I'm propelled by the Repeater, a hand cupping a cheek of my ass, fat fingers scrabbling at the seam of my underwear through the thin cotton dress.

'You don't remember me?'

'No.'

Naz might remember him but I don't – *Naz, where is*

Naz? He could help. When did he leave? – I want to erode this man's aura, make him small. 'You? You think I would remember someone like you?'

'You should. I kept you safe as a child. Kept all the filthy people out. Guarded your walls. We have the same blood.'

'I didn't ask you for anything. I didn't want to be guarded.'

'But I remember you.'

I want to scream out. My oldest friends are avoiding my eyes, they look so different, I don't know these faces. Nakul laid out on the ground. Aurie on her knees. She's sobbing, stroking his cheeks. He writhes in little starts, like an internet video buffering.

'Your husband was a violent man,' the Repeater shouts across the lawn. 'It must be in his blood. They only understand the same thing.' He kicks him once swiftly in the side. 'You think you can take anything?' he asks, looking down at Riz.

'What d'you want with us?' I shout. 'Please. Anything. What can we do for you?'

A Repeater comes up from behind. 'We were told you have a daughter.' Skin hangs in folds around his eyes, as if he never properly sleeps. It's only me and this man now. No one else is important.

I take a step towards him, bring my hands together, stare deep into his face, offer a look of love. 'Please, sir. She is innocent. Please.'

'I know she's innocent,' he says. 'That's why we're taking her.'

'Don't, sir, please. Don't do this.'

'She will be taken care of.'

My head is spinning. I can't break my thoughts into words. A vision suddenly of Leila running towards me. A long low moan emerges, again and again. Dipanita has come to my side. I am leaning against her, I fall to the ground. In a few seconds, when I come to my senses, my friend is being dragged away. She is screaming too. Three Repeaters have gathered for a conference around their leader.

'She's not there.'

'What do you mean?'

'That photo the brother sent. No girl upstairs looks like that.'

Their leader is looking at me. 'Where's her maid?'

'We can't find her either,' a Repeater responds. 'We thought they were hiding in the cook's quarters. But it was empty.'

The leader curses and swings his stick, hitting a tree trunk. 'Idiots, all of you. Take this one to the truck, whenever it gets here.'

Four men are carrying Riz. He stares at me, apology in dull eyes. Still I haven't understood what is happening, what has happened. How can my husband go for tomorrow's big meeting with his face bruised up? Mishra, his manager, will come to get him in the morning. What will I tell Mishra?

They are taking Riz away. In my last sight his face is horribly contorted, someone familiar but not who I expect, like a sudden glimpse of yourself frowning in a mirror.

Then I am alone. Leila is alone. I have failed in my only work, my single charge.

Glass of water. I must have a pill.

PURITY CAMP

It is not something from me but something of me that has been taken. The part that could feel warmth, happiness, desire. Perhaps I have yielded something of myself.

The truck drew up to a metal fence so tall its upper panels bent reedlike with the wind. Half the sky blotched like old carbon paper. The Repeaters sat by the truck's cabin, facing us. We were on benches with our backs to them, staring out the open canvas flap of the truck. The party was already blurred, locked in an obscure past. But for a few moments, or less, shadows pressing into my mind like a hot iron: the scarlet gash above Riz's eye, it won't stop leaking, mud, hair, blood caking his face; Leila upstairs and under the covers, whispering to her best friend, thrilled, ignoring the movie, ignoring me; her cake was a house, a home, smoking chimney, curving path, crosses for the window frames. Her birdlike hands in mine we pressed down with the big plastic knife into its heart.

All night the Repeaters clanged their sticks, their quivering rods, against the metal truck frame. They gave us no water.

I hardly noticed the engine's din, the heat from the metal floor. Only later I felt the blisters on the pads of my feet.

I held on to one thought, a single delusion, I see that now. It ran through my brain, incessant as the chain of white stripes that halved the road and slipped out from under the truck's carriage into the black gulf behind us. The delirium: I could turn this truck, turn the stripes, this very road. If I turned this truck around, I could make it back to the party, to Leila and Riz, to how things were. Leila could spend tomorrow opening her presents. Riz could still go to his meeting. We would celebrate by going out to dinner. If I could just find my home again, Riz would come back, Leila would be there. All I had to do was get back home. As the distance between us grew I began to feel a deep pressure in my shoulders, a resistance band, Leila, Leila holding on as they forced forward.

A tear reached the corner of my mouth, warm and thick with salt. One woman had pissed herself, wetting the plywood bench. At first I jumped to the side, a reflex action. Yet it hardly seemed important. With perverse detachment I felt my dress wicking the liquid, smearing onto my thigh. Another young woman sat against one side of the truck, intermittent in the road lights, a naked face, shorn of the daily artifice – displaying every vulnerability. She stared ahead unseeing. It felt as if I'd caught sight of myself. We came to a gate. Along its length the fence had red skulls on signboards promising electrocution, but above the gate there was no sign, nothing to mark the fork in the path.

The darkness lifted with a stark grey light lining the brushwood and the fields of scrub earth. We were fourteen women, most young, around my age. One girl had a bandage on her shoulder blotted red and iodine-yellow. When we climbed out of the truck the long blue sheath I was wearing tore. More flashes from the party, again with that sense of distance: the maid laying out choices on my bed, tentwaalas erecting orange and red shamianas on our lawn. Leila lifted her frock up to her waist just before she cut her cake, everyone laughing, everyone singing. *What had she wished for?*

As the sky paled to pearlish blue the birds woke, swooping and soaring in the drifts, their freedom inimical, ludicrous. The Repeaters took us from the truck to a mud yard outside a small white building. They had us line up on our knees. The flaps of my dress rode up my thighs. My arms and shoulders were bare, goosefleshed. But morning brought relief, a sense that the danger had passed. When the sun is up men remember their responsibility. At night they will do anything, as if their vileness, their desperation to possess, can only be seen in the day's glare.

We were vulnerable – the loose, the ripe – choosing sex over family, over the wishes of the elders, the intentions of the community. Through the night the Repeaters had prodded us with their sticks, finding a fleshy thigh, a side of stomach, thrusting in the splintered end.

We waited on our knees. The woman first in line was shouting. As they dragged her into the building she began to scream, round, lupine yowls. This isn't her fate. It was never her fate. I tried to get my bearings. The compound was surrounded by low hills, granite and coppery mud, from which jagged chunks had been quarried out. Even now you could see two yellow excavators biting at the earth like Cretaceous birds grubbing. The excavators pushed out thick red clouds. I sensed already, that first morning, that this was a place apart, separate from everything else. Even months later, any sign of outside existence, of things going on as they always had – birds, a motorbike on a distant ridge, dynamite from the mining, the reports pinging around the hills before landing in our basin – always seemed strange, unreal.

A vision comes. Leila walking on a broad, empty road. Her back is to me. I feel my panic rise. Thrust the sight away. But it returns, insistent, finding a chink to slink through like smoke.

A strapping nurse in a long white smock and loose pyjamas came up to us. She was the biggest woman I'd seen. Six feet tall, each forearm like a clothes iron, carrying a huge plastic bottle of water, its slender neck between two fingers like it was no weight at all. Condensation fogged the plastic. How thirsty I was. We all leaned forward in anticipation. The nurse walked to one end of the line. 'No wasting,' she said, and in turn poured a stream, silver from the sun, into the cup each woman made with her hands. She was two places down from me when someone grabbed her knee.

'Where are we?' this girl asked. Her voice was gone. She'd cried through the night. A mousy thing, so thin her slim-fit jeans sagged at the buttocks. 'What is this place?'

'All questions will be answered,' the nurse said.

'Wait,' the mouse quivered. She tugged at the nurse's smock wretchedly, like a beggar. 'You don't understand. I have to go back. You have to take me back.' The nurse had an indulgent smile. A woman to my left let out a guttural snarl. 'Let her come down the line, goddammit.' Grumbles of agreement. 'You'll find out soon enough,' the nurse said. She freed herself, continuing down the line with that same smile. The girl broke into sobs.

The water was sweet and cold, an icy current into my chest, taking my breath away. I drank until the nurse stopped pouring. After that I could look around once more.

There was an L-shaped structure, four floors – from the evenly spaced windows and doors, up and down, clearly a dormitory. A water tower with an enormous crack along the equator of the cylindrical concrete tank. Further, past a stand of thorn trees, a gabled shed built like a barracks, with dozens of windows almost kissing the ground. The Repeaters who'd made the night journey with us were walking towards this shed now, each carrying a little backpack. They were everywhere. Flanking the building in front of us, patrolling the perimeter, on the roof.

A group of women dressed in white emerged from the dormitory led by a pair of towering nurses. In silence we watched them perform a callisthenic routine. By the time the guard came for me my knees were pounding from the inside, a steady bloodbeat radiating out. The sun was high in the sky. He put the toe of his boot on my thigh. I ignored him. He grabbed my elbow, yanked me up. My knees stung so badly I almost crumpled to the ground. I fought him away. It took me a minute, but I walked myself into the small office building.

==

An open-air corridor with a number of shuttered green doors. In the middle room a bald man sat behind a desk. He had horn-rimmed glasses and a rather timid smile. An air conditioner hummed. Sweat had soaked the back of my dress, making me shiver. The Repeater pointed to a wooden chair with a sagging jute string seat, then silently withdrew.

'I'm Dr Iyer,' the bald man said. He extended his hand casually, as if I'd walked in off the street for a consultation. No photographs on his desk or the walls. 'Was your journey okay? Some of the measures . . .' – he searched for the right word – 'they're unfortunate.' A grave shake of the head. 'But necessary. Very necessary. Understand? Tell me, when was your last period?'

'My what? What is this place? Where have you brought me?'

'We call this Purity Camp.' His smile brightened, turning beneficent. 'It's for you all.' He poured himself a glass of water and drank it in a gulp. 'Your last hope.'

What does that mean?, I thought. Mistaking my gaze, he pressed a button on the desk. 'I'll get you a glass,' he said. Then he opened a drawer and took out a gleaming wooden box, the size of a notebook, with a miniature nickel latch. 'Do you know why you're here?'

I tried to keep anger from my voice. 'You call yourselves fancy names. But I know what you are.'

'You don't understand,' he said. 'We will end these cycles of violence. Restore equilibrium. Order will be there, and purity.' He flicked open the latch with the nail of his index finger. The box was lined in burgundy velvet and contained blue and white pills. He scooped up a few, presenting them on his open palm. 'Do you know what these are?'

They had a faint smell of plastic. 'They'll help you sleep. Help you find peace. We synthesised them with great effort. Ingenuity. Because we care for you.'

The nurse walked in. She held a tray with an empty glass, and, dangling from her broad wrist, in a clear polythene bag, a new pair of thick-soled rubber slippers atop a folded set of clothes. 'I don't believe you,' I said. The doctor gave a sardonic laugh. He dropped the pills into the box and took off his spectacles. He was like a frog now, eyes too big for his forehead.

'You don't have to believe me,' he said finally. 'But you have to believe someone. Who will you believe, Shalini?' A mild smile replaced the bitter laugh. It made my blood boil. 'Don't you know,' he said, 'we're the only ones left. The only ones you have. Believe or don't believe. But there's no need for me to lie. Why would I bother?'

I may have shouted. I may have got to my feet.

'That won't be possible. Not now.' He spoke calmly. Hot tears needled my eyes.

'You know what happened. I wasn't there. I haven't spoken to anyone. But even I know what happened.'

I wanted to leap over the table. Get hands around his neck, squeeze until the life left, bury teeth in his flesh. 'Where's my daughter?' I shouted. 'Leila! Why were your men searching for her?'

'Your daughter will be raised properly. For her sake. We want an ordered society. Parents like you, she would never see the value in our way of life. Never fit in. Don't you want her to fit in?'

Tears dropped down my face without check. 'You don't have her. You don't,' I said softly. 'She was saved. She hid. She saved herself.' I tried to wipe my face with my shoulder. My skin was filmed with the dust of the road, my thin blue shift a belch of truck smoke, under my arm old sweat like vinegar.

'Right now you have too much anger, Shalini. It's okay. Don't cry. I can understand, I can understand.' He pointed to the clothes and slippers the nurse had left behind. 'Why don't you get comfortable? I'll wait outside. Don't worry. No one will see.'

I needed fresh underwear, but I went to a dark corner away from the windows and changed into the starched kurta-pyjama. I folded my dress, held it to my face. In its weave I searched for Riz, searched for Leila. On a sudden impulse I left it on Iyer's desk, before his empty chair. Part of me wanted to keep it, but that dress wasn't any more for me. We left the building from the side, crossing the vegetable garden. Iyer shouted at a dog – 'hoouwf, hoouwf' – until it charged away. The four women I'd left kneeling in the dirt in front of the office were still there, roasting in the sun. I couldn't care. I had to find out anything I could about Leila. What they intended, how much they'd managed to do already. Dr Iyer wouldn't say. As we moved across the loam fields I felt like a child, asking questions in tow. I brought her up time and again. He would return an enigmatic smile and keep moving. We came to a small scrub forest where the trees looked like barbed wire. Months later I followed a woman we nicknamed Lady Police to this very grove. By then I'd become so accustomed to life at Camp that a sense of curiosity, a need to pry, had returned.

The water tower stood alone at one end of the compound. Still, we were almost there by the time I realised it was Iyer's destination. I assumed he wanted to talk about the water problem, though walking all this way seemed a strange amount of effort in the heat, unless Iyer preferred effect to comfort, and he seemed too soft, too plushy. It turned out the tower had been dry many years. Dr Iyer used it for something quite different.

We pushed through a low gate. A sprinkle of rust came onto my sweaty palm, glittering like sushi roe. This small enclosure was overgrown with brambles, various nettles.

Someone had dumped long twists of barbed wire. Iyer stepped carefully through the vegetation, pointing out half-buried wire jags as he went. A staircase snaked around the massive pillar-base, its steps cracked and sooty with age. The railing was gone. Only the spokes stood, every four steps, rods of blackened, twisted steel. Iyer hopped onto the staircase. He looked once to see I was following, then began a speedy ascent. The climb was scary. I tried to stay as close as possible to the pillar-base. Some of the steps were broken in half. Many were missing altogether. As we went higher, in a number of places two steps were missing in a row, and we had to jump without looking at the dizzy emptiness below, trusting ourselves, trusting the concrete not to crumble underfoot. Iyer turned out to be nimble, faster than I expected. We kept climbing. The wind picked up. The air wasn't as dry up here, no longer a hot-sand scrub. Gusts came strong and frequent, jiggering my each step. I was frightened. I called out to Iyer but he wouldn't listen, so I decided to slow down. Essential now to be more careful than I'd ever been, to remain safe, healthy, simply to remain. Leila was at the mercy of these delusionary men. She needed me to find her. The railing appeared, briefly, gone within a dozen steps. It felt like a missing crutch. I couldn't bring myself to look down but I knew how high we'd come. Already we were above everything save the surrounding hills.

Finally we came to a parapet that wound around the base of the giant tank. We must've been a hundred feet up. The parapet wasn't broad, only two feet, though here at least the railing remained. Suddenly it all caught up. The day, the party, the Repeaters, the price they took. I felt drained, every muscle frightened. The wind was wicked now and my head spun from the height and exhaustion. I began to crawl, inching along the parapet, three or four steps on my hands and knees, my new kurta snapping in the wind like a mast. But crawling also felt dangerous because the railing was higher than me. If a gust suddenly grabbed hold I would go tumbling out beneath it. With my palms on the curving tank, I got to my feet. I tried to take a deep, slow breath but even that was short-lived. As I stood up I grabbed the railing, which rattled alarmingly. For a terrifying instant I thought I'd gone over, but the railing just vibrated in its groove. Tremors travelled along the railing, right around the water tank. Iyer heard. He came around from the rear, walking casually, looking out to the horizon, a hand shielding his eyes from the sun, like a pudgy little sailor up on a ship's crow's nest.

'Do you like the view?' he asked.

I had my back flat against the concrete tank. 'Is that why you brought me here? To show there's nothing around us? Nowhere to run?'

'Tch, tch. You're thinking too much, Shalini. You must put away your anger. That is why we've come here.'

I wanted to scream in his face, but I couldn't step away from the wall, relinquish the security of it at my back. I had to calm down. Only then could I speak. 'What did you expect, Dr Iyer? Tell me, how should I act?'

'Be angry. That's what I'm saying. That's why we're here. We call this Anger Tower.'

'What do you mean?'

'It's my solution,' he said, beaming. 'Do you like? Whenever things become too much. When you're remembering your daughter, your husband. You come up here.' He pointed down to Camp. 'Here you can do anything. The nurses down there, they don't allow too much talking, complaining. If they catch you crying you'll have many problems. But come up here and you can shout. Abuse as you want, kick, scream. You can even abuse me!' He made this last proclamation as if it were an absurdity.

'You think it's that easy. That all of us will just put it aside? Just like that?'

A squall of anger suddenly rolled across his face. 'All of you? Ask the girls in your truck. The rest know. It's only you, women like you. You grow up thinking you are already abroad. Some TV-world you live in. That such things are your right. But see these girls you came with, girls from different places, ask them. They won't be surprised. They knew what they were doing when they chose to live this way, what risk they were taking.

They don't act so shocked, like you do. They know there are things bigger than themselves. Rules bigger than themselves. That's why I brought you here. Go on. Shout, scream. You will only stop shouting when you see it's your fault. You didn't understand the first thing about your own home, your own life. They accept. You want to fight.'

'You're crazy,' I shouted. 'Old and crazy. You don't know what you're saying. They're just as angry as me.'

'You will see for yourself, Shalini. I don't have to tell you.'

With that he walked to the stairs. He spun around when he reached them. He had a prim expression, a placatory smile. I realised suddenly that he wanted me to think him a good man. 'There is no question of extirpation, of course,' he said. 'We aren't animals, like some. But you will stand as a symbol. An example. You must show the rest.'

I stayed there alone some time, trying to calm down. Below was stifling, the air unmoving. It felt good to be in a breeze. Good also to be so close to the edge, the narrow, rotting parapet and wobbly railing and tremendous height. I realised this later. On most days at Camp I felt our separation as a physical hollowness. But up here that long numbing ache was replaced by a rush, my body reminding me that I had work, that I needed to go on. This place sharpened my senses, my mind, burnt a path through the shadows closing in. Much of the time at Camp I felt exhausted, but not here. To be a single step away from death made me feel alive.

Was it that first morning, up on the parapet, that I made my list? This is what memory suggests. But I remember also the weakness of my mind in the first weeks, how everything seemed a muddle. Was I clear enough to make this list, to hold it in my head? (I didn't dare put such things on paper.) The list I made:

More Info Needed:

  – They hadn't found Leila when they took me.

  – How can I get word to Mummy?

  – Where did Sapna go?

  – Was it Naz? Could it . . .

We slept in a long room on low bed frames set on concrete blocks. They kept the fourteen of us together for most things. Meals, group sessions with Iyer, Purity exercises, gardening duty, clean-up. I learnt to properly sweep a floor with a jhadoo, down on my haunches. Learnt not to be revolted by the stiff black rag they gave to mop the floor with, the filth in the corners. Evenings I swept and mopped the four floors of the dormitory. At night my knees felt on fire. For the first time it occurred to me that no one – not Riz, not I, our friends, family – had thought to buy long-handled brooms and mops for our homes. Did we enjoy keeping these women's noses to the ground as they cleaned? We brought in televisions and cars and phones and everything else from abroad, why not these simple things?

By the first night alliances had begun to form amongst the thirteen others. I didn't know how to join in, where to. They seemed so different. A few spoke no English at all. At first the rest treated me with something like deference, but as time went on in Camp, and the congruence of our routine, our circumstance, became clear, those differences seemed to matter less. I farted one night just after we'd gone to bed, thinking it would make no noise. For a few seconds there was silence. Then Prarthna, the mousy girl, started laughing, and soon we all were.

Prarthna was in truth far from mousy. She was a tough little thing from one of the Kayastha sectors. It was she who first opened up, talking as we lay in the dark, staring at the ceiling of this queerly elongated room. She had bribed a judge to marry her to her lover, a woman she'd met on the production line in a car factory. They claimed to be roommates and rented a place in their own sector. Both sets of parents had grudgingly accepted their choice. They lived quietly, happily. Six months on things began to change.

'Someone was whispering in my parents' ears,' Prarthna told us. 'I know who. My father began coming to our flat when my wife wasn't there, begging me to leave all this, to come home. He was a good, gentle man. Never bad to me or my sister. He said my mother was being shamed in the market, on the street. It was difficult for him at work too. People had somehow found out. They wouldn't let it go. I refused. So many times he came and each time I said no. We had our own problems, I told him. Still he kept coming. Once he even warned me. He'd heard that our elders were aware of my situation. That the Repeaters were prowling.' She broke off, cleared a catch in her throat. 'I didn't believe him. I thought he was saying it to get me back home.'

All those women were tough, tougher than me. Iyer was right. They knew what they were doing, they did it anyway. I thought we were safe because we were well off, because we knew important people. These were strange and beautiful women with the courage to slash at every expectation. There was one girl from the Haryanvi Jat sector with light brown eyes that danced with the sun. Sonam was strong and fit and tall. She fell in love with a boy from the same village, the same gotra. Their community had retained many tribal traditions, such as this strict forbiddance of love within the clan. Sonam would walk with her boyfriend to school. By fifteen they knew no one would accept their relationship. One day they went down to the railway tracks that ran along their hutment. Young couples from their village, sure of their love, unwilling to contemplate life beyond it, stood at a curve on these tracks, clenched together until the train scattered them into a thousand pieces. Sonam and her boy walked to the tracks, stood at the fated curve, felt cleansed by the cold breaking current of the great engine and its load as it hurtled by them. They decided to run instead, to hold on to their love. The Repeaters found them in a station hotel.

We were all curious about the girl with the big bandage. An expression of confused sadness had claimed her face. I can't remember when Vasanthi told us her story, it must've been a while, because the bandage was gone by then. She was a Thevar girl who'd fallen in love with a Dalit boy from her college. 'We were at the bus stop. Earlier my husband's family would come with us if we travelled, to keep us safe. But after one year of marriage we decided it was safe to travel alone. They were in a gang. Hacked him to death. They held my arms and my head and they made me watch as they chopped at him with axes and swords. My brothers were there. Father too. One Repeater thrust a sword into my shoulder. After that I don't remember much. After that it was the truck.'

It is a litany, a litany of our shame. There was a Muslim girl who'd run away with a Yadav boy. Elders from both communities sent gangs after them. A Yadav girl who'd run away with a Dalit boy. They made her watch as they force-fed him poison. Night after night I felt weighed under, as if these stories came from every side, demanding submission. There was a chubby girl with wet, red lips, Sana, who looked different, younger, less sure of herself. Later I realised this was because she was a virgin. Sana had been so quiet the first days that I couldn't tell she was like me, well spoken, well brought-up. Bohra Muslim. She hadn't found love outside her community like the rest of us, the elders had chased her out.

One day – the hottest we'd had – the two of us were weeding the vegetable patch. Maybe it was the heat, or the work we did, the garden fork's gleaming metal prongs, the digging, uprooting, the flat plate of the hoe slicing again and again into the loose earth. Sana decided to tell me her story.

'People hated me. Since I joined college they hated me. They said I was too smart. You know how they say it?

Smerrt. She is too smerrt. As if it's an insult.'

'Because you went to college?'

'Not that. That the elders like. It makes them feel they've been very benevolent to us, to the young women. They're proud to let us go. It puffs them up. Look how it used to be. Look what we allow now. They want us in college, but they don't want us to think. That is what's dangerous.'

'What happened to you?'

'I had started a campaign against the khatna.'

'Khatna?'

'A very old practice in our community. They cut the girl's genitals well before puberty.' She stopped to mop the sweat off her face. 'I started a movement, demanded they end the custom. That's when the trouble began.'

'What did they do?'

'Everything in their power,' she said quietly. 'First no more college. Slowly, one by one, they turned in everyone. My mother had been against me from the beginning, but my father believed it was time for change.' Sana's fingers, halfway in the dirt, scrabbled against something hard. She pulled them out of the soil. Her nails and knuckles were dark brown. Picking up the trowel as if it were a spoon, she plunged it deep into the earth. 'They made his life miserable,' she said. 'No work. Named him infidel, traitor. They said all of us would have to leave the sector. That's when I went. I told the Repeaters myself. Take me.'

POLAR NIGHT

I don't like taking the bus in the evenings. Sitting at the bus stop makes me nervous. Gnats and moths make dizzy loops to my torch. I can't see the furry line of kikars in the distance. When the Council first sent us out here I could walk at night because there was hardly anyone around. Now I hardly dare. A woman walking the Outroads alone belongs to no community, no one. Fair game.

The bus appeared, diving and lifting with the potholes. A stream of red-eyed women exited the bus. A hunched girl, gaunt of face, pallu cinched tight around her waist. A young woman with a phone around her neck playing a film song. One lady only had one arm, her other limb veined green with muscle. None would meet my gaze, staring at the puffs of dust kicked up in front of them. Women recruited as day labour, most likely, working on one of the new construction projects.

Three men and a woman remained on the bus. I found a seat towards the back and began to rehearse my testimony. In less than five minutes my eyes were burning. I was reading through a blur. Over the years oval rims have bruised the tissue around my eyes, jagged ellipses of smooth, pink, slightly softer skin: raccoon eyes. You find them on everyone who moves about the Outroads, because the air down here is thick with particulates from the factories, cars, travelling smoke from the burnt sharecrops. The particulates itch slowly, they form a film between eyeball and lid. It's impossible not to rub the skin around the eyes, harder and harder, like each has been sprinkled with some fiery powder.

These rims around our eyes are a badge, a signal of the depths we inhabit. We try and get rid of them how we can. Cucumber, chamomile, milk and honey. Nothing works like water and baking soda. Earlier in the day I dunked one side of my face into a bowl and forced the eye open, rolling the salty solution around my eyeball. I repeated it with the other eye. It nibbled delicately, like a tiny fish. But it calms the inflammation.

==

Three people I've loved most of all. Daughter, husband, mother. I don't know where any now lies. Everything I do feels random, without real purpose. Like a balloon unstopped, zipping one corner to the other, every moment weaker, lesser.

When there's a news report from a Council school I burst into a panic. As details unfold the fear burrows deeper inside me. Abuse is rampant. One boys' school is buggering down the line. Teachers on students, seniors on the little ones. A flesh market on the premises of a girls' junior school. Begging rackets, mutilation, disease, drugging, theft. No one cares about the children in these schools, not really. We are a people of family, of community. When the parents go, aunts and uncles and grandparents step in. What kind of child has no community? Only those from the very end, the tattered last. Only children from outside the walls end up in a Council school.

Not Leila. Leila will be a lawyer. She is tall, like her father, like Ma, with pale skin and a still-raw garrison of pimple scars on her cheeks. One of this year's incoming students in the law faculty. Unless she's gone another way, an artist, hair sensibly back, kameez careless at her shoulder, dabs of dried clay on her arms and neck and chin.

Ma? She is dead. Dipanita told me that years ago. Did they cremate her? Send her down a river? Did they perform the rites or throw her away? Her body, the way Dips described it: cold in a cold bed, lips pale from the poison. And Riz. Is there a chance? If he were alive, they'd have told him I was dead. He would have no way of knowing. He could be living in a Slum. Maybe he also looks for Leila. Maybe he's forgotten me.

==

The conductor was at my side, a young man not more than five feet tall but firmly built, with a gleaming coal stripe for a moustache. He walked with his chest out, strutting his small frame. I felt a spike of pity. Years of pubescent despair, waiting to catch up with the taller boys, taking a hard job at a construction site to build strength. His khaki uniform smelt of drying fish.

'Political sector,' I said.

He looked at me with new curiosity. 'This time of night?' He inspected my plain white sari. 'Didn't you get on at the Towers?'

'Yes.'

'Eh, madwoman. No offices open now. Where do you really want to go?' He scanned me from top to bottom. 'You're going to meet friends?' he asked. 'You have friends there? In the political sector?' It took a second to realise his stilted hiss was laughter.

'I have work.'

'But no offices are open. What work?'

'I don't have to tell you, do I?'

'Only if you want to get dropped. Go on, press the bell. See if we stop.' He grinned down openly. His teeth were small and white but horribly crooked in the lower jaw, like pickets of a beach fence that are cudgelled each dusk by a sturdy wind.

'A tribunal. They called me at this time. I have no choice.'

He took a sharp breath and a tiny step back, the smile gone immediately. His eyes furrowed. He seemed about to reach for my shoulder. 'No charge,' he whispered, and hurried on.

On reaching the city proper, the first wall you see encloses a smaller sector, for Salsette Catholics. Every morning as I ride past I see a sprawling crystal palace, like something from a fairy tale, the early sun shimmering off the wall's grey scales and the church steeples and the mirror plate office buildings that rise like uneven turrets. This late at night none of that is visible. Giant advertisements, each between two or three storeys high, bounce with blinding lights. The adverts are bolted to the wall, seedy proclamations and petitions for custom that charge like rutting bulls along the road and then right to your face. Afterschool Home Tutorials; Ahurmazd Gastric Bypass; Tip-top Maids (Choose religion, caste, birthplace; Be Safe Be Tip-top).

Relief when our bus turned onto the Outroad adjoining the East Slum, away from the manic messaging, though the Slum is a noisome meld of human waste and rotting vegetables. Stagnant water fed upon by a scum of mosquitoes. The Slum pressed in from either side, only a crooked sliver of road remaining that the driver wended down. As we took a corner a man squatting across the gutter alongside the road sprang to his feet, brown eyes flashing when the bus's double beacons washed over his frame. He fumbled with the waistband of his trousers. By the time we rumbled past he'd scrunched fabric into his fist and held his trousers above his crotch, looking away with a nonchalant air.

We completed the turn. A dazzling sight as soon as we did. A sky the shade of a monsoon sea. The clouds light and white, without burden, floating cumulus islands. I slid the window to see better. Slum stench braised my cheeks and neck. I didn't care. You never see a sky like this any more, not with the thick smog and hanging industrial effluent. This sky was better than any I remembered. Instantly I was driving along an open road with Riz, early spring, the school year just done. Craning to read, once again, the blotted-ink farewells the class had scrawled over my uniform. The sun turning his hair brown and gold. A sense of contentment, of completion. The clouds were different that day, a wide translucent stretch broken into tiny ripples that covered half the sky.

This seemed to be some kind of advert. Blackness hung like a roof, and below it a layer of daylight and day cloud, an Arctic anomaly, a polar night.

As the East Slum petered out I saw what was being sold. On a panel towards the top of the wall – high enough to be seen from the flyroads – white text stood on the sky: 'Must Your Children Share Their Air?' Centre of the last panel, again in white letters, the corporation's name, Skydome.

==

Now I wait my turn outside the tribunal room. I'm in a building in the far end of the political sector that faces the running track and the duck pond with the low white-brick fence, a charmless structure with porthole-style windows that proved very difficult to find. The roads in the political sector arrow into roundabouts and one another, they confuse me terribly.

How different everything is as soon as you go through the Great Gate, as if a switch has flipped. My job brings me here every day so I see it all up close. Wide, lovely avenues, empty of pedestrians, fringed either side with a stripe of thick boscage, palm squirrels and macaques skittering through the leaves. Every home is a sprawling white-walled bungalow encircled by hillocked lawns. In the morning or evening, walking between the Ministry and the bus stop, the pavements are all but empty, and for once, with everywhere so much green, I can take in great, open lungfuls of air. The deep breaths make me light-headed. I calm. I appreciate better the singing birds, the abundance, the tactile rejoinder of my feet on the pavement. Each square tile sits in deep grooves. It feels like a different world, a fathomless distance from the place I live, on a mountaintop, perhaps, locked away. The political sector is the prototype. One by one, so I'm told, all the rich sectors have begun to look like this.

This sense of emptiness is amplified at night, and the contrast with the outside, teem and glare and revolting profusion. I scurried between the bows of dusty orange light from the street lamps, anxious for the whining zip of a car, any sign of life. Every few minutes I'd reach the inlet to a driveway, leading up to a low gate. Just beyond the gate a green wooden shed-post bearing two slumbering machine-gun-men. It wouldn't do to ask them for directions, so I kept walking. I saw a porcupine and the glowing yellow eyes, round and lovely as planets, of a slender loris. Most of the rustles and shivers in the branches I sped past with head firmly down. The important thing is that I've made it here on time. It has just gone 10 p.m. Three men and a square-framed woman in a sari sit with me in the waiting area. She is rocking gently while reading from a sheet of paper, mouthing the words as she memorises them. Though it's a cool night, though the fan finds me every few seconds, my scalp, forehead, the pits of my elbows and knees, everything is slowly leaking. If they don't believe me, I'll go like the others. Never to be seen again. Salt stirred into water.

'Could you stop that?' the man at my side says. A thin smile. 'Jiggling your knees like that.'

He accepts the apology with a curt nod. I've spent plenty of time in corridors like this. A caged fan mounted on the wall scans corner to corner. The panels of the prefab wall behind me judder each time someone comes up the stairs. On the wall opposite there's a houndstooth of grimy rectangles where notices were taped up and then less carefully ripped off. The false ceiling is missing one panel altogether. I see red wires and for a second the shadow of a scuttling rat.

He leans over, lowering his voice. 'Actually, I'm nervous too.' Buried in his breath is the tang of dinner, pickle and potato and paratha, a big start before his big meeting. A vermilion teeka sits like a splotch of fire on his forehead. 'But they're not *that* scary.'

'Have you been to a tribunal before?'

'Just tell the truth. You have nothing to fear.'

I smile weakly. My stomach feels as if someone has scooped it up like ice cream. Still I sweat. I lift my handbag to my lap and root through it until my fingers land on glass. The jar's rubber seal yields with a belch. Blue and white, rocket to delight. Vital for confusion, distress, panic, other forms of fear. They stink, these pills, the nauseous upthrust inevitable every night as if a trigger in my stomach is flicked by the pill's descent.

I stare at the spherocylinder in my palm, blue neatly slotted into white. The first time I took this pill they had to hold my jaw open like a dog at a vet's. I mistrusted everyone, especially Dr Iyer. Now we know he was one of those who hoped to help. One morning after breakfast this blue and white pill was at my elbow in a plastic cup the size of a wind-up toy. It seemed to have suddenly materialised. Not many of us took it that first day. It was easy enough to secret away. I used the elastic band of my pyjamas. Later I emptied the capsule into the sink and washed down the powder and shrivelled plastic coat.

The man has spotted the pill in my hand and is glaring. He drags his chair away. Its legs scrape the stone with a sound like fabric tearing. 'Where do you live?' he asks, then repeats himself.

'Erm . . .'

'She's from the Towers,' he announces. Three faces look up immediately. He leans in to inspect, bathing me in prandial reek. 'I've never met a Tower woman before. No wonder you're so nervous,' he says. My ears are hot with shame. With a satisfied smile he explains to the room, 'I knew it. Only they take those blue and white pills.'

It's the curiosity that irks, as if I'm a specimen, requiring study and support. For the most part we aren't confronted with anger now. Instead we face these sudden transformations of demeanour, of regard. What meaning I once had has been taken, converted. I don't give a damn.

I toss one into my mouth as they gape. Then I wait. Warmth climbs in slowly, through a ground-floor window. A buzz in my calves, the first flurry. It feels for a glorious second as if my body is completely loose, like I'm draped over something, shaped into a smile. Cold bubbles fizz against the inside of my skin. The room begins to softly breathe. The overhead light has burst like a rainbow into fluid shafts of colour. I close my eyes. Maybe they stare, but I no longer care.

A new beginning. If all goes well in the tribunal, if I get the transfer, I will never again have to see the people I've worked with at the Revenue Ministry for so many years. I haven't made friends there. I go to work, carry tea and papers from office to office, clean as I'm told, come home. I don't want anything else.

Is it lonely people who are mad or mad people who are lonely? For some time now I've picked at this fear like a scab. Why is the loon always alone, taking the streets in solitude? So many years without Riz, without Leila. Maybe I no longer have the firmest grip on things. I first considered this possibility at work one day. I'd entered the kitchenette to make the morning round of tea. Pinned to the cabinet that holds the cups and saucers, so I was sure to see, was a pen sketch on lined notepaper. I'd been drawn with my nose in the air. Shalini had become Baalini, so the legend announced, with stretched locks of hair springing straight out as if I'd been shocked at a light socket. The caricaturist exaggerated the slight protrusion of my front teeth so I scowled witchlike. In between each curl (my hair isn't that curly) arrowhead squiggles sprang from my skull, representing my temper, which I suppose was out of hand those days.

But the point is not about the drawing, the irritation I felt, the laughter it must've inspired in my colleagues. At the time I had no way of knowing how angry I'd become. I might've shouted at one or two peons. Maybe I'd suggested to the Slummers who came to sweep and mop that I wasn't meant for this, that I was from a good family, this work too manual, too menial. Some of them were so stupid, getting the simplest things wrong. I'd end up screaming. But until that morning I saw that drawing I had no real awareness of my behaviour. I'd imagined myself as collected, as self-possessed as anyone. The caricature helped me realise. I have become unmoored. Without Riz by my side I'm losing control. Now it's hard to know what my own mood is like. Riz was a guide, a centre, he helped me gauge what I felt when too tightly wound. This is why I worry. The loneliness of these sixteen years is taking me out of myself. I will edge into a different state without realising.

A peon yanks me out of my reverie with two sharp fingers into my shoulder. The same four people look at me with open contempt, like I'm a junkie. I stand and open out the middle finger of my right hand. Before anyone can notice, or at least object, I follow it with the forefinger. Both fingers on my chest, smile around the room. 'Purity for all,' I say.

The tribunal room is dark wood, fusty, oblong. There are no windows. Concealed lighting leaves much of it in arcs of shadow. Four men at the far end are sunk in discussion, each in the white dhoti with the single near-invisible orange stripe that the Council's senior functionaries like to wear. At the creak of the door they stop talking.

'Sorry,' I say. 'Should I wait outside?'

'No need, no need,' says the man who broke off mid-sentence at my entry. He looks at his colleagues. 'Let's get started?' He walks towards me, squinting through the gloom at a folder in his hand. He stops and lifts a palm. 'Wait. You are from the Towers?'

I assent.

A smile spreads across the man's face. Behind him three leers. 'She's from the Towers,' he says, as if he's making an announcement. An overhead light flicks on in the far end of the room. There is a bed. A *bed*? A high bed, like in a doctor's office. The light casts a neat triangle upon it, a bolster pillow at one end, covered in the same silk, black as pitch. The day Leila was taken they lined up like this. The afterglow from the pill floats away.

'Why don't you lie down? I am Mr Vijay.' At a signal from Mr Vijay the peon emerges from the shadows. Without any instruction he arranges four chairs around the bed. They will sit, two each, at my torso, at my thighs. A flash from a documentary, a movie maybe, Japanese women stretched naked on tables with sushi arranged across their shining satin bodies, so diners can slaver over the topography of their vaginas, the ridges of their knees, the smooth scalloped breasts. I adjust my blouse. The peon walks away. The door moans and for a few seconds the light improves. Then the quick snap and slide of a deadbolt.

Walking out before the business is complete means no transfer to Settlement. Without the transfer I won't have the address I've hunted for since they took her. As I hoist myself onto the bed I let out a small sound, something like a whimper, that echoes off the wood, making it bigger than it was. Making me smaller. One officer laughs. He has a stuffy nose. The four take their seats now. Each is a foot from me. Their faces are in the dark but four sets of thighs in translucent dhotis shine in the light from the bulb. Knees and bare shins. Be brave, brave for Leila.

The first questions are straightforward. Confirmations of name, age, Tower number. Then the man at my right knee says: 'You must know – we don't give transfers to Tower women?'

'Yes. But I was told sometimes . . .'

'And why should we do such a thing for you?'

'There is simply no question,' Mr Vijay interjects. Thick rings on each of the fingers on his right hand, even the thumb. The stones look like traffic lights in the murk. 'We don't give to Tower women. How could I send you to Settlement?'

'I want to prove my commitment to the cause. I would like to show you.'

'What more you want to show, madam?' someone says. 'Gergh gergh gergh.' Then Mr Vijay asks, softer, 'How old are you . . . ' – a rustling of papers – 'Shalini?'

'I'm forty-three.'

'Oh. You look older. But still beautiful. What do you think? Isn't she good for her age?'

Bile at the pit of my throat. The underwire of my bra is cutting into the incline of flesh. Shifting around doesn't help. I use a fingernail to adjust the point of contact and there is a quickening in the air, the breathing around me harder. I stare at the ceiling and will the minutes away.

'So, Shalini . . . ' – Mr Vijay's voice trembling like a weary muscle – 'you were one of those women. You went against family. Against society. You could not control yourself. For carnal reasons.'

'Yes, sir.'

'I can smell it on her,' another man says. His finger lightly traces the curve of my quivering waist. 'It's still in her, even at this age. Mixed with the other smells. In her sweat.'

'When woman gives in to carnality,' Mr Vijay continues, a choke in his voice once again, 'imagine if all women gave in. You know what will come? Utter confusion. Bedlam. We are a society that needs rules. Boundaries. The ancient lines are there for a reason.'

'Yes, sir.'

'You were a good girl. You broke from your own people. From your community. What good can come from mixing like this?' He rolls a sheet of paper into a tight cone. He places its point just above my hip. 'Look at you,' he says, almost whispering. 'Your skin shines like a pearl.' He presses the cone sharply into my waist. I bleat. 'Even after all these years. So beautiful. No wonder they were angry.'

'Please believe me. I know my mistake. I have learnt my lesson.'

Mr Vijay moves his hand to my sternum, and my arm shoots out as a reflex, like a windscreen wiper, across my breasts. All four are smiling now. I sense it despite the darkness. This is what they do best, these powerful men, inject vulnerability.

'How long were you in Purity Camp?'

'Four months. With Dr Iyer.'

'That's a long time,' the second voice interjects. 'Why did they take so long with you?'

'I don't know, sir. I was confused about many things. I didn't want to listen. Dr Iyer helped me understand.'

'And what did you understand?'

'That the walls are important. We must have them. The whole city used to be like the Outroads. Lawless. Filthy. Dirt at your doorstep. People shitting on the roads. Into the gutters. The best people could not live like that any more. We needed the walls.'

'See how beautiful it is now,' Mr Vijay says. 'Everything so clean. Our network of flyroads known all over the world. From Singapore, America, everywhere they're coming to see it. One community to another, above all the mess. Would it be possible if people did not respect the walls? If everyone lived like you – against their own culture, against our culture?'

'I come here every day. It's very beautiful.'

'I know this.' Mr Vijay's face is dimly visible in the penumbra of a shadow. Eyes dart across the top of the papers sheafed in the folder. 'In the Towers you have to live amongst it all, but that is your fault. We did not want that for you. You chose to go your own way. What were we to do?'

'Yes, sir. I understand now.'

'There is no hope for the people on the ground, you know. They were like this a thousand years ago. They will live like this forever.'

'Purity for all,' I say.

'Purity for all,' they reciprocate.

'It's not just the dirt, Shalini,' Mr Vijay continues, leaning back. 'We need the boundaries for peace. Businessmen kidnapped for ransom. Rapes. So many women raped all the time. Now such things happen only on the Outroads. Families can keep their women safe.

How many people used to die every festival. Remember? What food could be eaten. What dance could be done. Mischief-makers taking panga in each other's localities. Swords and sticks and guns coming out. A lower man running away with a woman from a good family. They'd burn his whole family, his home, land, everything. Now every community can do what they want. If you respect the walls there are no problems.'

His finger sidles suddenly up my wrist. The cold metal of his rings is hard on the flesh and I let out a gasp and kick out in surprise and see in his smile that he's confused fear for pleasure. The swell in his dhoti will not sit. It's done, I tell myself. Almost there. The man with the stuffy nose had been playing with my toes, rubbing his fingertips across the desiccated sideskin. He snarls when I kick out. Mr Vijay stares for a few seconds at a point above his colleague's head. Abruptly he stands. 'Out. Everyone. Out.' He rests a hand on my shoulder to keep me in place. It feels suddenly like I've journeyed there just now, that I've been somewhere else all this time.

The buzz of yellow light strengthens and sinks as the men depart. Then we're back in the solitary cast of the light hanging above. Mr Vijay is smelling me, taking soulful whiffs. He is trying to place his head between my breasts, beads of saliva on his lips. 'I want to give you the transfer, Shalini. But there are complications.'

'Please, sir. I must go to Settlement.'

'You *must?*'

An icelike finger of fear stabs my chest. 'Sir, it's only . . . I've been waiting so long. I've understood now, what you want from us. I want to help.'

'I don't care, you know,' he laughs. His jaw rests on my breast, like a puppy. 'Go there, don't go there. It makes no difference.' He slides his finger underneath my bra.

'Then please, sir. *Please.*'

A shrewd light enters his eyes. 'I don't even care why you're so desperate.'

'Then what do you care for, sir?' Tears course down the side of my face. They splotch the bed sheet next to either ear. 'What is it that you care for?'

'Will I see you again? I want to see you once more.' The diction is jerky. 'Once more. Once is enough.' His right hand is tucked inside his dhoti and furiously hiccupping, the red and yellow thread on his wrist jumping in the dark. I close my eyes. 'Tell me fast,' he says. 'Fast-fast. When will you see me again?'

'As you wish, sir. It is your wish.'

'No!' he cries out. 'Not my wish! Not like that.' He looks down at his lap and releases an anguished moan. For a moment there is silence like after an echo, round, swaying, swelling ever further. He growls, 'Your wish. It is your wish,' and slaps a palm on my right breast. He twists the flesh, scrunches it like a crisp sheet of paper. He has my nipple between the tips of his fingers and his eyes are large as a fish on ice. The pain is roasting and pink. He looks half-crazed. Blood might spurt from my ducts. The right arm bounces even faster, the congress he conceals jittering the creases of his dhoti like an epileptic's collar. With each cry I make his left hand squeezes harder. He is tugging my breast every which way, clamping down and then easing his hold. 'Your wish, your wish,' he is softly saying.

'My wish, my wish,' I whisper like a whore.

He yanks the bra cup off my breast. It tears slightly as it strains against my back and he moans again and brings his face to me. He clamps down on my nipple with fleshy, betel-red lips, gnawing like a toothless person, through the fabric. His shoulders, neck, chest, convulse to the beat his wrist is tamping upon his thighs, into his brain, craving completion, as his tongue flicks in and out, rough as a mop against the tip of my nipple. 'My wish,' I whisper into his ear, and suddenly, without notice, he has shuddered to peace, forehead on my stomach, deep, laboured breaths, nose buried in my waist.

Vijay is at the far end of the room wiping himself with an inside fold of his dhoti when I open my eyes. He has his back to me. I shift my bra back in place. Hold my palm at my breast to dry the patch thick and clammy with saliva before I have to step outside. It doesn't make a difference.

'And regarding the transfer?' I ask. 'We will be meeting again?'

'What's that?' he asks, without turning around.

'Once again, you said. We will meet once again.'

'Oh yes.' He picks up a folder from the end of a table and studies it intently. 'No, that's okay. You can have the transfer. I'll see to it.'

FORBIDDEN FRUIT

My first week at the Ministry of Settlement. I've been given charge of room 401, a dim space with grey walls and eight rows of desks, four to each, like an examination hall. I make tea, wash the lunch plates and utensils, swab the oil smears and steam rings off the long table at the rear of the room. A late afternoon run for samosas. Dust the desks. Once a week unplug and shake out the keyboards to evict shreds of food and hair and skin. Sweep, mop, secure the windows against birds and monkeys. Then I can go home.

The stool they have given has no backrest. My legs dangle. I feel vaguely simian. The nasal lilt of an ambulance siren drifts in from the road. A young woman here looks just like Dipanita. She sits by the window, centred precisely in a square of sunlight. Once in a while a frizz comes loose and falls on the side of her face like a lash of laburnum, and when she bends to write one shoulder blade distends her back, sticking out of her sari blouse, like a shark fin emerging from a smooth pale sea.

She stands and stretches, unbothered by the men who turn their necks. This girl reminds me of the Dipanita I once knew, the confident crackpot I grew up with. Not the drawn, anxious woman I had coffee with one Saturday morning ten years ago.

==

Ten years ago. I remembered Dipanita's number at once, but I must have dialled it a dozen times before we actually spoke. It wasn't just Dipanita. All my friends. What I'd been through, I knew, was too much for any of them to accept. Things like this didn't happen to them, to us. My existence now was a threat to their idea of home. It would not do to plumb this depth. I pictured the reactions. Concerned but confused; a flicker of an embarrassed smile; warm, knowing nods when they looked properly upon my clothes, when they heard about life outside the walls, outside the city. I needed clarity. Not pity.

Eventually I held my courage. Dipanita sounded so excited to hear my voice. She said I should come to her place, they'd just redone the living room, and prattled on for minutes about a new designer sofa set. I almost disconnected the call in disgust. But I realised as she spoke that my call had made her nervous. Then she was angry herself. Six years. You don't even call? You know how worried we've been? What we thought? The angrier she sounded the happier I felt. It made me think that I was once again part of things, present in the moment, as if the years between were an interlude, a false loneliness. For a long time after we spoke I felt quietly excited. The next day I went into the city. I found a little shop on the border of the East Slum that served the neighbourhood children. The counter of this shop spanned the front, to make sure the crowd of kids couldn't touch the toys. The toys were themselves depressing, tiny wood-wheeled carts to drag around by string, dolls fashioned from wafer-thin plastic, blue eyes, pink-cream skin. Pressing a doll even lightly left an indent you had to pop out from the other side.

There are also shops that serve the ragged lowest sectors. Some communities have erected walls out of a sense of ancient pride but are in reality so poor they cannot sustain even neighbourhood markets, forget the marbled gleaming multi-decker malls the others have. The toy shop I found smelt terribly of milk, but here at least you could walk the two dusty aisles, handle the toys. Pari was two years older than my daughter. Eleven. Neither dolls nor dresses seemed right. Then I spotted, underneath a wooden shield, coated in dust, a small pink box with an envelope-style flap cover. One thousand fifty rupees. The cover illustration had a slinky woman in red high heels and knee-length sheath blowing on her nails. The back of the box claimed this was the ideal starter kit. It came with a small bottle of white nail polish, stamp, scraper, two stamping plates with flower, heart and star designs. I imagined her friends crowding around her, examining her nails from every angle.

The boy was two years younger. There was a child's cricket bat, shrink-wrapped, thick rails of dirt across the plastic. It looked poorly made, with a scuff of tiny white splinters above the splice, but I didn't have money for much else. When I reached home I dampened the tip of a cloth and wiped clean the packing. I wonder sometimes if Riz and I would've had another child. A young boy, my laadla, my prince, whom all three of us would cosset, feed, spoil. His nest of unruly hair, incisors too big for his jaw, a delicate paunch. He would play squash, just like his father.

I'd just finished wrapping the presents when my phone buzzed. Dipanita sounded like she'd been crying. Some part of me had been expecting this call. There was a problem, she'd explain later. Would it be okay if we met at a restaurant in her sector? I agreed at once. I could tell her husband didn't want me in their house. They must've fought about it. He believed I would bring the outside in with me, disease, filth, immorality. All of that is now attached to my person, to my eternal person.

==

One evening I sat with Dipanita in my living room. Leila and Pari were in a corner, laying out an imaginary meal on my daughter's Minnie Mouse tea table set. They came to us periodically to demand Riz blow up balloons for them. They would volley the balloons in the air and chase the bounce. Since Pari was older, quicker, Leila followed her everywhere.

I was spread out on a beanbag. Dipanita was on the couch and Riz in his armchair, smoking a cigarette.

'She's the fastest girl in her class,' Dipanita said.

'She's very tall,' I replied.

'Make her a runner!' Riz said, excited. 'Or a tennis player. She's got the height. I'm going to take Leila very soon. Tennis lessons. That's how they do it abroad. You have to start early.'

'Dips,' I said, 'at least applaud his optimism. Both of us suck, but daughter is going to be Steffi.'

Leila and Pari had been bouncing their balloons off the ceiling. Now they slowly approached us. Pari stood, hands behind her back, in the vacant space next to a coffee table. I thought she might recite a poem. Her right leg twisted behind the other. She looked down at the carpet with a shy smile. 'I won all the races in my Sports Day,' she said. 'Wow,' I said. 'Your Mamma says you're the fastest in your class?'

'I am,' she said, nodding seriously. 'Not just the girls. I beat the boys also. All of them. They all came after me.'

'Very good, Pari,' I said. 'Remember that when you're older.' I shot a sly look at Dipanita. 'Find a boy who comes after you.' The three of us were a beer in and we began to giggle. Pari stood perfectly still, scanning each of our faces methodically, puzzled.

'Yes, Auntie, I will.'

'I'll kill you, bitch,' Dipanita whispered, still laughing. 'Don't dirty my angel's head.'

Leila had silently watched us sink into laughter as we spoke to Pari. She misunderstood. She left the carpeted area around the coffee table and walked around the leather couch until she was standing a few feet behind my beanbag. She leapt at me even as I still laughed, wrapped her arms around my shoulders from behind, knees scrabbling across the pliant cushioning, clinging to me with all her strength.

'Someone's jealous,' Dipanita said.

Leila was giggling also now and trying to climb me. I put my arms behind my back, found a grip and heaved her around to my lap. I buried my face in her neck and vibrated my lips like a car motor, tickling and wetting her. She squirmed with a sense of our oneness, of the feeling we shared, that we were each in exactly the right place, that the world held nothing outside this touch. I felt her wriggle in my own bones. Leila still had then the comfort every child needs, it hadn't yet been taken, that her home lay in these arms, that here she was safe. She had flattened me onto the beanbag. I heard running steps on the carpet. Pari took a flying leap and landed on us and then I was submerged in tiny arms and legs and hands and feet.

==

Two days after we spoke on the phone, I travelled to the Gupta sector, a sprawling crescent swathe very close to the political sector, invitation in hand. Dipanita's letter had the formal typewritten note, with her signature, identification number, address and biometric mark. On the other side she'd written in pencil: 'Dear Shalini: Still in shock. Been trying to figure out ways I can help. Talked to some of the girls. We have to do something. Can't wait to see your beautiful face next week. All my love, Dipanita.' Despite myself, reading the note brought a thrill. Maybe this would end. Someone could be called. Leila inched closer.

Sunshine turned the polished black gate into an enormous mirror. This gate, four storeys high, operated at two levels.

By the ground pedestrian traffic filed towards it, the line progressing in minute spurts. Directly over our heads was the flyroad. The old cross-girders sent out a thundering judder every time a car went above. A mound of trash sloped out from the sector wall, covering the pavement and rain gutter, petering out at the edge of a row of huts. All the rich communities have a Slum roosted at their walls, where servants, sweepers and scavengers from the concomitant castes make their homes. The men and women in line with me had all come from these huts.

The clothes of the man in line in front of me were damp and musty like a sodden newspaper. I'm told this system works well. Earlier servants would sometimes have to change their names, cooks had to lie about their caste, their religion, maids claim they were born a rung higher so they could wash the dishes and swab the floors of the high-caste homes in their vicinity. That was before, when the city was haphazard, before order had been achieved. Now servant-shanties come up along the edges of the communities they've served for centuries. No one need cross the city for work or pretend to be what they're not. Riz's parents used to serve this special kebab, spicy, soft as a pastry, prepared by a thirteen-year-old, a bawarchi boy who came to their kitchen from the Qassab Slum outside their sector. They were happy to have him and he was happy to have such good masters. A fine system.

We were a few feet from the towering gate. I could see only some of the way up. The hinges were long, alternating triangles, tapering to a point about halfway along the gate's breadth, fastened with dozens of giant rivets. Paint hung off the gate in patches, revealing islands of tangerine rust. The hunched men and women ahead were showing identification papers. In turn they stepped through a Judas gate that opened and shut like a tiny winking eye. A fleshy, middle-aged Repeater, white shirt open to his belly, processed the documents of each of the Slummers with an irritated air. His forearm brushed wetly against me, clammy skin, sweat-curled hair. He read the invitation letter, looked me up and down. Reluctantly he pulled me from the line.

'Come this way. This line is not for you,' he said, heading towards the gate. Black and white chest hairs leaked from the U of his vest. 'Why have you come here?'

'Doesn't it say in the letter?'

'Never mind what it says. I asked you.' As he said this he turned and stuck out an arm at the chest of a tall fellow at the top of the line. The tall man had bent his neck preparing to walk through the Judas gate, but he jerked back at the Repeater's sudden swing. A gap opened up and I was angled through the inlet. The line watched without rancour.

'Thank you. The letter should explain. I've come to meet an old friend.'

'I will have to check.' He looked at the well-worn sandals, the dust lines on my sleeves from the railing on the bus. 'Guest!' he said. A sallow, sweaty palm upright to indicate I should stay. He walked to the guard booth, began speaking into a phone.

I found a high-shouldered ber and leaned against the trunk, on a gnarl like an enormous snail shell, keeping an eye on the guard shed. The flyroad that entered the gate thirty feet above us now declined, returning a river of metal-toned cars to earth. The line I had just been pulled from had cleaved in two. The women walked two at a time into a white shed with the curtains tightly drawn. The men filed into a narrow arrangement of canvas screens. There was no roof to the screens, so I could see the tops of their heads. A Repeater waited. One by one they pulled T-shirts and kurtas off over their heads and bent to remove their lowers. When they were dressed again they'd join one of the clumps of Slummers that had moved beyond the checkposts, making their way to a home, school, office, hospital, wherever they'd found a bit of work.

The guard is waving me on, pointing at the road I should take. Two or three minutes' walking and a green begins either side of me. Low hillocks, kempt grass, trees thrown one way by the wind like sails on an open sea. The lingering fingers of trash stink are gone. Now the smell of daffodils, fresh-turned sod, and suddenly, the wonderful pungency of aloo dum. Some families have laid out a picnic on a wooden table. A film song reaches the road. A servant boy, oiled hair shining, sighs open an enormous PET bottle of highlighter-orange soft drink. With both hands he pours measures into Styrofoam cups. The men are playing a game of cricket.

The road leads to a canal with swirling, murky water, pine-green in parts, alongside it a busy cycle and running track. Young couples lie fully clothed on beach towels in the broad strip of shade bordering the water. I descend from a footbridge into an open garden pocked with wrought-metal tables and chairs. This seems to be the place. Waiters in dress shirts, a trio of guitarists walking between the patrons singing Spanish Sinatra. I round them and find a table in the far corner, away from the families.

==

After Papa died my mother seemed to search for something. Every Sunday she went to a neighbour's house to listen to the sermons of a young man-god. She insisted on taking me. It was important we did this, she said, it would help us find peace. It wasn't easy for her. Riz was there for me but she had no one. I could feel her sadness all the time, almost like an aura. Even when she was doing the things she loved, it remained, an invisible, impregnable coat.

Sixteen or twenty people gathered in Mr Sharma's living room. Incense sticks burning in bunches made a thin cedar smoke. Ma and I were each given a red, linen-bound prayer book and a string of rosary beads. This holy man was slender, even undernourished, with high cheekbones that made him look slightly surprised. He sat cross-legged on a low platform at the head of the room, dressed in a grey homespun robe, a solitary set of beads around his wrist.

We followed the chanting with the group for twenty minutes, leafing through our books to find the right prayer. Then an apprentice came through the devotees. As the rest went on with their prayer he led Mummy and me into a small room, a guest bedroom, it looked like. When the apprentice left I begged my mother to turn around, walk out. Don't worry so much, she said, Sanjana Auntie told me about this part. We waited, as instructed, on a long rubber mat at the foot of the bed. In a few minutes he came in. He looked even younger up close. The door was shut carefully after him by an unseen hand.

As he lowered himself to sit cross-legged in front of us I could not help but wonder what kind of underwear he had on beneath his robe, if it was like the ordinary ones men wore or if the cowl, or his sainthood, demanded something else. He looked deep into my mother's face, then he turned his gaze to me. His face seemed to narrow. 'What took you so long?' he asked. 'I've waited for you your whole life.'

I gaped at him, unsure what to say. Ma stared with equal surprise. Finally, she sputtered, 'What do you mean?'

He gave us a serene smile. 'I've met you before,' he said. Both of us shook our heads. 'Tell me, do you travel a lot?' he asked my mother. 'Not now. When you were younger. When you just got married. Did you ever travel with your husband?'

'Not that much, but we did travel, I suppose,' my mother said. 'My husband had a motorbike. We used to ride up to a nice spot in the mountains, spend a few days.'

'I can see, now, that we met many years ago. It was a very hot place. No, not a hot place. A place that created heat. The air very cold but the ground warm. Have you ever been to a place like that?'

   'That could be anywhere,' I said.

'Your Papa and I did go once to a place like that,' my mother responded. 'To a village where there were hot springs. I'd completely forgotten. There was a young boy who took me right up, who showed me how to get to where the women were bathing. Was that you?'

The man-god had a calm smile. 'Indeed it was. I was an apprentice. My guru spent every summer in the springs. Did you know then that you were carrying this one?'

'It might have been when we were carrying her, yes. I can't be sure now. Maybe we had gone up to celebrate? But how could you have known, after so many years?'

'I have to know. I knew then. I know now. I knew I'd see your daughter again.'

Ma was ready to fall at his feet. It made me tremble too, the way he said that, such surety in his tone. But later I could see the clever trick he'd played on my mother, how the needed information was elicited.

When Riz laughed at me for believing, I argued. Riz had read Dawkins in America. You weren't there, you don't know, I said. If you were there you'd have seen it for yourself. He took me into his arms. That's the first thing everyone says, my beautiful girl. Should I believe the stories my mother tells me? Should I find you a sexy burqa? He laughed as I pounded him with my fists.

Dipanita is twenty-two minutes late. Her face shines from a moisture spritz. Her skin has changed, it's noticeably lighter. The only badge of age is a tilak-like double wrinkle on her forehead. She looks so shiny, so fresh, which makes me think of finality, the roundness of each moment. This was it. My only chance. I will never look young as she does at thirty-three. She's wearing a pale green sari, the blouse with a pumpkin-cut about her upper spine that displays a smooth white back. This is the first thing I say to her: 'You've become so fair!'

She stops where she is. For a few seconds she simply stares, eyes brimming. Behind her pastel lips a jumble of questions, then tears, hot on my shoulder. She is sobbing with such force that I start to cry too. An old couple gapes at us from an adjoining table.

'How has it been – where did they take you?' she asks. 'You look . . . you look . . .'

'Older?' I venture, with a laugh.

'No, no, you're looking good,' she says, turning away.

'I know when you're lying.'

She wipes her eyes, her cheeks, nods quickly a few times,

grips my shoulders and studies my face. She starts to smile. I feel immediately hot. Sometimes, when I look in the mirror, it seems like something vital has been drawn from me – a monster emerged from sleep and shadow and took to my breast and now I have begun to shrivel. I admit I do want sympathy. For her to grasp what I've been through. I remember a time being happy, for the most, about how I looked. Dipanita now is a reminder of the difference, the chasm between that old self and me. There have been moments when I forget, when I look up expectantly at an attractive man coming down the bus aisle. He walks by without a second look. I have this sudden urge to follow him, to whisper my real age, tell him I'm just like him. But I know now, from Dipanita's reaction when she saw me. No one cares. Even she, who can guess what I've been through. I feel cheated. It never really matters what brought us here. It matters only in what state we reach.

Dipanita releases my shoulders, though her eyes continue to cast about my face. 'You've gone grey,' she says finally, in a pragmatic tone. 'And there are lines above your cheekbones. Other than that you're looking good.'

'You look just the same,' I laugh. I put my arm against hers. 'Except for this glowing new skin. Look. We're almost the same colour now.'

She gives a strained smile. Absently, pretending she doesn't know what she's doing, she takes the sleeve of my kameez between her fingers and rubs it a few times, feeling the rough cloth. After the waiter has taken our order I tell her about Camp. The journey straight from the party, shoulder to shoulder with the others on wooden benches in the back of a truck. The stench of sweat and clothes soaked in urine. Every second the truck placed a vaster blackness between Leila and me, every second the panic mounted.

'They've made homes for them, Dipanita. Council schools. Hundreds of kids, no visitors. Where they learn only the Council's rules.'

'Can't you do something?' she asks. 'Show them the paperwork?'

'What can I do?' I ask. 'I have no papers. I'm all alone. Even Mummy is gone.'

'I heard about that.' A deep, hissing breath of regret. 'I didn't visit her, you know. After they took you. I'm so sorry.'

'Sorry? Why?'

'I should have helped. She was good to me.'

'That's okay,' I say calmly. 'How could you have helped her? You didn't help me.' She flinches as if I tried to hit her. 'That night, I mean. Even later. None of you did. Why would you help my mum?'

She looks down at her lap. Still looking down, in a low voice she says, 'What could we do? There were so many of them. You think we didn't try? That summer was crazy. No one knew what to do. Who to call.'

'In your letter you said you spoke to the girls. What did you mean? Were you able to think of something?'

'I did, I spoke to everyone. Talked to Atul also, after he calmed down. He was so angry that I spoke to you on the phone. That's how difficult it is now. No one can do anything. These people, they're running things in this way. We have to accept it. For the children, for our own sake. We can't take risks. Not after what happened to you.'

The small flame that had been trembling inside me since her letter goes immediately dark. 'Do you know what happened to my mother?'

'I don't know. I don't want to say. There were stories going about.'

'Tell me.'

'You remember Rasika? That girl from the Arora sector? She says Auntie took pills one night. Too many pills.'

If I suspected this I had never dared neaten the thought. A flash of her sitting upright in bed, eyes shut, white lips and blue skin. Maybe she blamed herself for leaving her granddaughter's birthday party when she did. But I told you to go, Ma. We were going to drink and dance as the kids slept upstairs. There was nothing for you, I told you to leave. Dipanita pours me a glass of water. 'Don't mind,' she whispers. 'Don't mind. That awful woman has nothing but gossip.'

I take a long draught, my eyes closed. This image of my mother is hard to evict. The coffee arrives. After the waiter has departed, I say, softer, 'I needed her when I came back.'

'What's that?' Dipanita says. 'I can't hear you.'

'My mother,' I say. 'She couldn't last. Not even the months I was in Purity Camp. I'd never do that to Leila. I can wait forever. I'm going to find her, you know. She needs me. I'm going to find her and be with her.'

'How?'

'I need you to tell me something. Promise me you'll tell the truth.'

'Of course I will. How can you ask that?'

'Does he have her? Naz?'

'*Naz?*'

'Did he take her? I know he called the Repeaters.' Dipanita rocks back in her chair in surprise. 'I just know it. I tried many times when I got out. He refused to take my call. I went to see him but the guards at the gate wouldn't let me in without a letter. He feels guilty, I know it. He'd become obsessed with the family property. Do you ever see him?'

'Here and there. Not really. He's become pretty political. He's a big guy now. I heard he took possession of your flat in the East End and sold it within the year. Atul told me once that Naz made your father-in-law sign over everything. He's something in the Council, too, now, a representative of some sort.'

A surge of anger. I realise moments later who I am angry at. Riz's carefree face hangs before me. How he misread his brother.

'Does he have her? Do you know anything?'
    'She isn't with Naz, Shalini. How would he have her? I know he has two sons. I've met them. They look just like him. Just like Riz. They haven't got Leila.'
    'There's another possibility. I heard one of the Repeaters at the party, just before they dragged me away. I keep going back to what he said.'
    'What was it?'
    'One of the young guys. He came running to the leader. Told them Leila wasn't in the house. That Sapna, our maid, wasn't there. What could that mean?'
    'There was so much commotion. They brought the kids down, made us all leave. But that leader guy was very

angry. Kept shouting into his phone. Kept sending men upstairs to look for something.'

'Do you think . . . they didn't find her? That Leila managed to hide?'

'My kids were fast asleep. They don't remember anything. Where could Leila have hidden? They turned that place upside down. Where could she have gone?'

I take a deep breath, closing my eyes. If Naz does not have her and the Council could not find her, there is only one other possibility, a single road to my daughter. Noises from a construction site carry softly to us. The drone of metal sawing stone. A series of hammer strikes, seven or eight in a row, the gap between them suggesting the hammer's great weight. The sizzle of welding torch on steel. The sounds cycling, as if one person moves between each task. 'I heard something else,' I say, my eyes still closed.

'Yeah?'

'That Repeater, telling his boss. He said *the brother* sent a photo to them. Of us. Of Leila.'

'The brother?'

'That's why I think it was Naz. Unless it was some kind of code, some designation they had? But why would they? It had to be him.'

'My god,' Dipanita says. Her hand goes slowly to her heart, as if I've paused its beating. 'Are you sure?'

I feel blood rush to my face, hear it swirling in my ears. 'Sure! You think I'm sure of anything now? Nothing makes sense. Everything I think back to, everything is so vague. Like some black dream. Sometimes things happened one way, sometimes another. I wake up in the morning and I'm not sure the day before was real.'

'It would explain what happened to their family.' She raises her right hand to her face, each finger curled back at the first joint. There is an oval ring on her third finger with a portrait of a man-god against a black background. 'God was punishing him,' she says, and in a smooth, practised motion puts the ring to her chin, lips, nose and forehead.

'What do you mean?'

'It was really very sad. It even made the news for a couple of days.'

'What happened?'

'When Riz's dad died, they buried him in the family graveyard. The family was Barelvi, I think? But the priests, some local leader, someone said that he wasn't from their zaat, their biraadiri.'

'Yeah, they were Barelvi. So what happened?'

'Naz was new to the Council then. Atul says he let them do it, refused to object because it might lose him the vote. But maybe he couldn't have done anything.

You know what it's like when these people get their fire up.'

'I don't understand, what did they do?'

'They dug him up one night. Can you believe that? Accused him of all kinds of things. Worshipping in temples. Said he didn't care for their zaat. That his family broke the rules. They dug him up. Sent the body back to the house in an ambulance one night.'

I can't bear to listen. Shame curls into me. It feels like we've let him down. Riz's father was so proud, a tall, stern man, much darker than his sons, with a sweep of white hair old age had not breached and a tiny flap of umber skin dangling from the outside of his right pinkie. Abbu refused to have this removed, he called it his lucky sixth finger. Things got so bad between Riz and his father after we moved away that in the last years they didn't speak at all. But Abbu had never kicked up the fuss he could have. He would quietly send money for Riz's business. Maybe that's why Naz was so worried. He could see Abbu still loved Riz.

'He was always so dignified. So commanding. All his life. I can't believe they would do that.'

The waiter is back, asking for a selection. Every item on the menu is written in light green. On the top right corner of each page are three Purity Stars. I decline another coffee.

'How is Atul? I've brought something for the kids.'

'What was the need, Shal? Really. They're so spoilt already.'

No one has called me Shal for a long time. It feels comfortable, though also strange. I hand her the polythene bag with the gifts. At the corners of her lips a gloat flickers. Look at these offerings. Or is it a different smile? Satisfied. She is the successful protector, her nest undisturbed. Dipanita hoists the plastic bag onto her lap and pulls the cricket bat out.

'Anshu loves cricket,' she says. 'He'll like this. I keep telling him there's no point.'

'No point?'

'No one from here makes it to the team. Everyone knows. The selectors have routes. They know who has the best fast bowlers, which communities produce the batsmen, best fielders. Atul tells him the same thing. He has to concentrate on his studies.'

She extracts the pink box from the plastic bag and turns it over in her hands, eyes widening at the woman on the flap. 'This I can't give.' She looks up. 'Pari isn't this type of girl. Her father would never let her use it.'

'Type of girl? Come on. We had nail polish at her age.'

'You don't know how important it is now. We have to bring girls up the right way. That's the main thing. Everyone is watching. Comparing. Until a good man takes her away we have to be careful.'

'Careful how?'

'Can you blame us? Look what they did to you.'

'Ah. That was my fault, was it?'

Her face is wide with guilt. 'Shalini. You know that's not what I'm saying.'

'What are you saying?'

'Atul tells me all the time. That's why I couldn't call you home. Community is the most important thing nowadays. Those fancy ideas we had as children, of love and pleasure, adventure, those are bad words now.' Her arms, crossed next to her coffee cup, are trembling, rattling the table delicately. 'We can't bring our children up like that. We have to be careful what the neighbours think. Meeting you was risk enough. That's why no one would come today, not one of the gang. We aren't allowed to meet Tower people, you know. It's too much risk. I just can't. I won't bring any risk to my kids.'

Something that she said earlier, something I must ask about. The guitar trio approaches. The man with the guitarron is grinning at me, the swollen back of the instrument bouncing against his hip as he walks, gums

— 203 —

stained with ringworms of paan juice. On the front pocket of his uniform 'No Tips Please' has been embroidered. Dipanita sticks an angry arm out and waves the troupe away.

'There is one thing I want you to do for me, Dips. Don't worry, it's not so bad. I want you to get in touch with Naz.'

'I haven't spoken to him in years, Shal. I can't just contact him. Things aren't the same. That kind of thing doesn't fly any more.'

'Then get in touch with Gazala. That might be better, actually. She's a mother. Maybe she will feel something.'

'What do you want me to do?'

I take a deep breath. 'I don't even have a photo of her. Not one photograph of my baby. They just dragged me away that night. They didn't leave me anything to remember her by. What if one day I can't remember her face? It frightens me so much. It makes me panic. I start freaking out. *What if I can't remember?* What if the details are already fading? Her neck, her cheeks, those small hairs before the hairline – do I remember them exactly like they were? All it takes is a little bit. Little here, little there. What if some day I'm remembering the wrong face? I need you to do this, Dips. They'll have something, maybe in an old album. Maybe they took the photos that were up on the walls of our apartment. Ask Gazala. I only need one. Just one photograph.'

Dipanita's eyes are screwed up, shining from tears. 'I'll see what I can do, Shalini. I might have one myself. That day we drove out to the hills for that picnic. Atul took a lot of photos that day. But I'm not sure which ones we still have. I'm going to try my best. If we don't have one, I will ask Gazala. God,' she said, bending to dab her eyes with the napkin on the side plate, 'I promised Atul I wouldn't see you any more. This was it. He made me swear. But let me try. Let me try.'

I know immediately that I'll never get the photograph. Already she struggles with the weight of what I've asked. It is too much to expect.

'There is one thing,' she says suddenly. 'That day . . . that night they came. A few days after that we found this little plastic shovel among Pari's toys. You know those bucket sets they sell for kids to take to the beach? It wasn't Pari's, I was sure of that. My maid thought we brought it back by mistake that night in all the confusion, that it got put into our bag. I could never throw it away because I thought it might be, you know . . . Did Leila have a beach set? Is it hers? I can send it to you.'

I cannot speak. Riz is carrying Leila into the ocean, her first time. I'm a few steps behind with a camera. She looks at me over his shoulder, confused, frightened, about to wail. Later she is plopped where the waves turn to rolling foam, doughy thighs sunk in the silver sand. I am crying again.

'Yes, please,' I say. 'Please send it.'

The waiter is appraising us as he walks over with the bill. He quietly places the leather folder in front of Dipanita. 'And Atul. How is he? You haven't told me anything about him. About your own life.'

'Atul is fine, I guess. His business is doing well.'

'I'm glad to hear that, Dips. I'm glad you're happy.'

'Happy?' She laughs unconvincingly. 'I wouldn't say that. Atul . . . thinks he's smart. But he's stupid. He's having an affair.'

For the first time there is something like defeat in Dipanita's eyes. Resignation. 'I'm sorry to hear that, D,' I say. 'Are you sure?'

'Yes. His secretary.' Her eyes are suddenly wet again. 'She's such a bitch to me. Acts superior. Won't pass on messages. Won't return my calls. Doesn't do any of the work I give her. And when I tell Atul he starts shouting, asks if he is supposed to fire her, as if I'm the one who is taking advantage. She comes from some shitty place. Had a tough life, by all accounts.'

'Really?'

'I think that's the fun now. All these fucking boss men. Forbidden fruit and all. As if their pussies taste different. No question of getting married, so it's perfect. All the fun and none of the hassle.'

A paddleboat shaped like a white swan ventures down the canal in long zigs and zags. Two young men pedal, puffing from the exertion. One of their companions is draped over the boat's gunwale, trailing a lithe white arm in the water. Dipanita slips a few notes in the bill folder and suddenly stands up. 'That's why I did it, you know,' she says. 'This skin whitening thing. I thought it would get him interested again. Long procedure. And bloody painful.' She laughs again, that same pained burst. 'Silly me. I really thought it would help.'

I remain seated. 'Will I see you again?'

She looks so worried, wringing her hands. 'It's difficult, Shal. Very hard. I'm going to try to talk to Gazala, of course. But I don't like lying to my husband. It's the kids, you know. He'd throw me out if he knew I was staying in touch. I can't endanger them like this.'

I stand up and walk around the table, put my arms out for a hug. When we embrace I feel her tears again. 'It was good seeing you again, Dipanita,' I whisper. 'It really was. Go home to your kids.'

SETTLEMENT

The girl ignores me. Never smiles as she goes past at the end of the day, as some of them do. I briefly considered the possibility she was Pari, Dips's daughter grown up. But they would never send her here.

Her name is Advika Chauhan. I read it off a postage label. She's Agnikula Rajput. I knew by the thread on her wrist that she came from one of the better communities, but it is clear Advika's family isn't wealthy. Her father will be a building darvaan, a security man in a factory, something similar, clinging to the edges of the sector from a time-worn sense of pride, but too poor, in truth, to pay the Council taxes, the rocketing property rates. This is why they send her all this way for the few thousand rupees she earns every month.

The hemp thread wrapped around half an inch of her wrist is bright red interwoven with yellow. Left wrist, meaning she is unmarried. In the political sector we have people from all around the city. The threads let people know where you are from. There are different colours for each grade. I look down at my own wrist, so thin now the bones might be ganglions, bony and bare. If you live outside the walls, like the Slummers or us Tower women, you aren't accorded a thread.

Advika adjusts the angle of her computer monitor. Through the window behind her a patch of road is visible. Pedestrians, the ridged grey bonnet of a parked sedan behind an interlay of leaves, along the pavement a strip of smooth, grey tarmac upon which every few minutes some ministerial convoy travels, a channel of bulbous white cars, the middle with a wailing red beacon on its forehead. Perched on my stool I have time to stare. This morning there was a paunchy, dark man with gold chains, talking into a cell phone, one hand flung out like a ghazal singer. Two ladies bundling forward in heavy silk saris. A powder blue suit who bent to adjust his shoe. Each person who walks into this snippet of shining white sun is untouched, blithe, unburdened by what transpires around them. They follow the thread of their day, think through worries, chase desires. They are allowed to grow, create. They needn't consider what goes on beneath their roads and outside their walls, they can section it from their minds.

Somehow Leila has stumbled into this square of spring sunshine. The Council did not find her. She has never known its choking grip. For this I would give anything.

Today I will have the address. This afternoon, while everyone is at the Sealing. My journey is coming to its end.

==

A fire rages in the East Slum. Seven weeks the landfill has burned. The Harnagar landfill is one of four mountains of garbage along the cardinal edges of the city, each growing higher every day. Harnagar is the biggest. It stretches a kilometre each way, rises further than any sector wall, any Ministry building, something like two hundred feet. On my way to work the bus takes me right past the blaze. The odour is unmistakable. It settles on your skin. Rub your thumb against the tips of your fingers and even with eyes closed you'll see black grains of the things that heavy this air.

Mummy would slap my hand if I held my nose as we drove past a stinky area, a sewer, a Slum, some other accretion of horrifying smells. A disappointed light would enter her eyes. 'Think of the people who live here,' she'd say. 'But they can't see us,' I would protest. 'What if they did it to you? Would you like that?' Neither of us could imagine I would some day have an answer.

If it goes well today, I will have a chance to teach Leila this little marker of respect myself. A message down from mother to daughter, without interruption, like hair carefully plaited. If it goes well today. Give me this, just this. Please.

The landfill ignites every summer. The firemen say the trash throws high concentrations of methane in the air. Usually the fires are small enough to be controlled. This time was different. The unseasonable sun sparked off the methane. In seconds blue-orange flames forked down from the brow of the hill in four distinct channels. Finding fresh fuel at a giant crag of hospital waste – needles, oxygen cylinders, blades, glass pipettes – over the ledges formed by the rusted bed frames, round and down the scarps that descended from a long, narrow plateau of non-processable plastic. On the first day of the fire the clouds were so thick the crows and kites and gulls deserted the skies. Cows, buffalo and cattle egrets once roamed the crest of the mountain, burrowing long faces in the loam with glee. Now they are gone. Of the scavengers only the rats and humans remain, hardy, hard to dislodge.

==

It's just past noon when the phones go off. Thirty-two short trills, from every part of the room, at precisely the same moment. My own phone is silent. I don't receive the same broadcast message. Every protocol, every computer system is calibrated to these sensitivities. Our message comes a minute or two later, in tow, bent low. Trucks leave for the Sealing at 3 p.m. sharp. Lateness will not be tolerated.

At fifteen minutes to the hour I pile into the bed of a truck along with the peons. I'm so excited I hardly notice the rush of people climbing in after me until we're about to get moving and I'm pushed up against restraints approximating a side wall, thick wooden planks set like a stile into the metal frame of the truck bed. The stile reminds me of childhood drives on rain-torn highways, stuck behind a cattle truck, two broad, black, muscled rears trembling down at me, their faeces-streaked tails swishing road bugs away. The truck gargles to life. I grab hold of a plank and hang my head over a strip of lumber so I don't have to smell everyone else. The inside carries a whiff of grain, or coir, fibrous and dusty. I'm very nervous. Under my breath I mouth a mantra. No Repeaters, no Repeaters, no Repeaters. Alongside the anxiety something else, when I think how it will be to finally have my daughter's address in hand, a cold, coiled thrill like the beginning of love.

A wiry boy, maybe from the hills, his eyes are like coin slots, pushes through the crowd selling amulets and charms. The black threads are looped around his right arm so the pieces dangle and when the truck sways the grainy blue and green and red stones catch the sunshine anew like glinting snake eyes.

Dr Iyer once told me that the right charm, a periapt of his choosing, would align my future. We were walking that afternoon on a path that ran alongside the boundary of Camp. He called these sessions 1-2-1s.

'The stone will be shaped like an egg. Bigger than a hen's egg. Like a swan's.' It was extremely hot and there was no shade. Iyer pulled a handkerchief out of his pocket and mopped his temples carefully. 'A pearl from the head of an elephant.'

'Which elephant makes pearls?' I asked.

'One in a million. That's what makes this stone very, very rare. I have read your charts. This is the solution. Find this stone and you will once again find happiness.'

I stopped dead, turned to him. 'How can I?' I shouted, anger clouding my brain, spilling out. 'All of this, what's happened to me. You want me to be like you? All this is because people believed in ancient stories.'

That is what I wanted to say. Instead I kept quiet, didn't break stride. We walked in silence, each breath going down like a hot draught, sandals crunching in the brittle topsoil. When I was calm, I said, 'Look what they did to me, Doctor. How can I believe such things?'

'It wasn't believers who did this to you, Shalini,' he said. He nodded slowly, voice soft. 'Someone with true belief is gentle. Pious. Those men were not believers. They were simply a consequence of that moment. Once in a while even the gentlest hand must ball into a fist. This is what they were. They were the fist.'

'We just happened to be caught in the swing?'

He shook his head as if disagreeing. Suddenly he shrugged. 'Things were worse before the walls,' he said. 'People fought each other, burned each other. Not just about women. Over who will get government money. Who will get jobs. Fought over everything. We were like animals. With the walls we have order. We will finally have peace.'

For how long?

==

Our truck is in a convoy moving towards Purity Pyramid. In ten minutes we are at the onyx monstrosity, winking and wavy like a mirage in the afternoon glare. It has a white tip. A balcony runs all the way around this tip, a viewing gallery from where the Council looks over the city. Purity Pyramid has been built at the precise centre of the political sector. It rises one hundred feet. Around its base a square of trim zoysia, every blade polished by the bright afternoon. We Tower women are not to come too close to the pyramid, but I know that the tiles, outsized mirrored half-hexagons that interlock, with grooves the depth of a man's arm, reflect an array of blinding blacks. This is why it seems to wink.

A stage has been erected on the grass upon which senior members of the Council stand in diamond-white outfits. We're taken up a series of tunnels. There are so many of us, all footsteps and murmurs. When we emerge once again into the open the audience below looks like ants. Repeaters herd us onto a broad, curving parapet built against the external wall of a parking lot. Below, Ministry workers dismount from air-conditioned buses and mill about confused. Bumping antennae, sniffing out the other's identity, their role in the colony. When they identify their area they hurry towards it, the relief in each stride palpable all the way up. This is what it is. When order and hierarchy break for even a few seconds, insectile panic.

Behind the stage a series of giant screens, together showing a baby-blue sky with broad swathes of carpaccio cloud. The signage is familiar. As we stare the clouds turn into letters, a word resolves: Skydome.

At ground level a chant has begun. 'Whyyyy share-the-air?' the audience intones. The heat makes their song gruff, blunt. They keep at it. 'Whyyyy share-the-air? Whyyyy share-the-air?' Over this, gradually, a distant clangour, clunks and clashes that sound industrial, suggesting size, coming from above and around us and growing louder by the second, like we're driving towards the roar of the ocean.

The Sealing is about to commence. Dholak boys pound skin before the audience. Each sector has a pair of these drummers, sweltering in embroidered sherwanis. Their insistent rhythm wheedles into the shoulders and necks and arms and finally feet of the long column of people behind them. The corporation's chant, over the muscular drums, reaches us in fragments now. A young girl with kohl-stroked eyes begins a slow, rhythmic dance on a wooden platform on one side, across from her another in the same black and gold sari dances like a reflection. In the great circular fire pit the first embers, big as boulders, warm to a tangerine glow. Priests are at carefully spaced locations around its circumference, like numbers on a dial. Behind each cowl a long line of people. When the believers reach the priest they hand over polythene packets. Coconuts, clarified butter, flowers, fruit tumble into the craggy licking flames. In one zone, men in flowing kurtas and beards and knitted skullcaps wheel their black-curtained women in a square perambulation. Others stand, sit, bend double to the ground with an uncertain cadence. In another section, a procession of men and women is kneeing its way across the gritty road, up and down a channel, following a lady wielding a cross high above her head. The reverences leave a sour taste, the hypocrisy of their piety – it is hollow supplication, they rule as gods themselves.

I need to get moving. I pick my way through the crowd. Already it's a squeeze up along the parapet. Four Repeaters are tasked with watching us. Two in the distance, eyes on stage; the other pair is more worrying. My progress elicits complaints, elbows, flickering fingers. I stop when I'm close to the entrance leading down to the tunnels. The Repeaters are walking in a broad circuit, eyes sharp on the long strip of menials for any sign of unrest, any low cussing. The din thunderous as the two translucent halves of the dome come together. They are maybe a hundred feet apart. There's a chill in the air, ice-cold currents taper down from above. The air conditioning has kicked in. Shrieks and shouts, joyful, entranced. Around me Slummers and the Tower folk delight in the sight, though they will return to their shelterless life every day, no prospect of sleeping under this cleansing second sky. The audience below breaks into a holy hum. The Repeaters stare straight up like the rest. Fast as I can, I slip through the entrance.

I negotiate the tunnels without incident. On the road I

begin to jog. The priests take their time if they feel the gathered are not sufficiently pious, if they haven't collected enough money – but to rely on this would be foolish. A huge roar chases me down the tunnels as the citizenry celebrate the completion of the Sealing. They have once again made a pretty package. This dome has majesty. Near see-through, a latticework of plastic venules across the sky. The grey pall that hangs day and night over the city is transformed. Where the sun catches the curvature right the light comes in rainbow drifts.

The streets are empty with everyone at the Sealing. As my feet pound the pavement, running free, wisps of dirge-like proclamations float over from the ceremony, announcements and claims.

Why share the air?
  PureSeal.
   . . . outside impurities.
  100% ClimaControl.
  Breathe easy.
  Cool breeze. Dust-free.
  Imported tech.
  Tell your Council rep today!

I slow to a walk just before the turn into the Ministry of Settlement, mop the down of droplets on my upper lip.

The air conditioning is glorious, a triumph. It makes me feel special, as if I've blunted this heat myself. I am restored. Ready for the Repeaters. Steady breath and open heart.

Even their attention is held above. A young, twitchy man examines my papers. While he pats me down he's goggling at the roof. Holstering his security wand, he straightens; there's childish excitement in his voice, as if he might suddenly start clapping, when he asks why I'm not at the Sealing.

'I was just there,' I say. 'I was sent back.'
   'By whom?'
   'Minister-sir. He has asked me to bring him his new camera. He wants to remember this day.'

He makes way without another word. Is the world suddenly different? Everything refreshed, colours rich, snatches of birdsong. The Repeater is smiling, he doesn't gripe at some needless thing. Already breathing is much easier, without the gritty chestburn that accompanies deep inhalation. The air has chilled beautifully, evenly. Behind the Repeater two colleagues are unbothered by my presence, one with his legs on a facing chair, tunic open, head all the way back. Everyone enjoying this splendid advance.

==

The things Leila and I will do together.

1. Oil and comb her hair. She will have long, difficult frizzes, like me. I want to rub oil into her scalp. Bunch strands in my palm. Stroke unguent deep into each one.

2. Factory Dhaba, in the East Slum. Formica tables and tube lights. Women can have a beer here without much trouble, the waiters keep an eye on the men. I hardly drink now but I must hear everything. What music she likes. Colours, whom she's loved, how she spent these years. She will be facing a stranger. I must be ready for that.

3. Buy her a dress. This is tricky. The good stores are inside the best sectors.

4. Travel to the East End. It's a sector now for Mohyal Brahmins, small but prestigious. They won't let us enter, of course. But she must see where she was born. If we can spot it, the home her father bought, how we once were.

5.

The Records hall is a long room with rows of blue-grey metal shelves that reach the ceiling. They block the windows, even at this hour the room gets only a gauze of natural light. A low ceiling, damp walls, air that clots your breath.

One end of the room a bank of ancient computers by a wall, each screen grubby with prints. I've been sent up to Records before on small tasks. This is the first time the room has been empty. The computers and air conditioning are off, leaving vacancies where there should be familiar sounds. Each rattle or creak is like the moan of the door: someone will walk in, yank me off this chair, throw me in lock-up. Sunder me, at this last step, from my purpose.

I power on one of the computers and pull up a swivel chair. A buzz of blue light, and a wheezing, strained drone that breaks the quiet like a dying electric saw. The programme that stores the land records is clunky. These machines needed replacing years ago.

The biggest problem is I can't remember her surname. We never learnt surnames. I remember so many things about the people who worked in our homes – quirks, scars, facial details, tics. But what came after Sapna? It is my understanding – perhaps this is wrong – that those born in the Slum never truly have a family name. They've lived outside society for millennia, nothing to pass on, why have a name other than the diminutive given by parents? I have a notion I saw the surname Kumar on whatever scrap of identification Sapna showed when she came to work in my house. It means prince, chaste. Sometimes they adopted Raja, or Rani, king, or queen. The irony is rich.

The computer has a file on its desktop named Harnagar. I open it while waiting for the records to load up. It's a report from a delegation sent by the Council to the landfill. They want to see what can be done about the fire. Smoke from the conflagration is travelling across the city in thick white clouds that extend unbroken till the horizon. Residents of the sectors neighbouring the landfill complain of chronic pulmonary conditions, eye trouble. The blaze spreads like a bush fire. Firefighters quell it in one place, only to find it has been sucked under the surface, flamed out elsewhere. A new layer has been added to the shroud of particulates over the city.

There are fourteen Sapna Kumars. I'm working down the list, crossing out names as I'm certain. I must get back to the Sealing before they miss me. I must figure out which Slum she has settled in, which sector it serves. If she lives in the wide arc of Slums adjoining the industrial sectors, that will complicate matters further. I check current professions, income levels. Then the penny drops. Only two Sapnas are listed with daughters at the right age. This is what I should've been searching for all along.

One address seems right. Sapna is in Harnagar. Hut 86, Mahaan Nagar, East Slum. This has to be it. Her girl is nineteen, exactly the right age. But why would she be at the landfill? The Sapna I knew wasn't from the scavenger caste. We wouldn't have let her tend to our daughter. Things must've been very hard for her after. Maybe no one would give her a job. Why else would she have descended to this, to scavenger level?

The other Sapna's daughter is eighteen. Strange. She lives right here, in the political sector: 23 Officer's Circle. The houses there are for the Council's highest echelons, top of the ancient ladder, the cream of society. I note down the phone number and address just to be safe.

So I must travel to the landfill then.

SAPNA

I'm hiding in a tiny sweet shop in the East Slum. I came in to ask for directions when a commotion began behind us. Quick as a monkey, the owner ducked behind the counter. I elbowed a customer out of the little shop and put my back against the wall. The stink of milk is making me gag, but I can't go out onto the road. The Repeaters are here. They're taking people, looks like it doesn't matter whom. Men, women, they're grabbing them off the road and tossing them into a blue van. The morning is very bright. All over there are puddles, grey, simmering lakes. A goat roped to a mailbox is watching me and chewing.

Someone tipped the Repeaters off. I saw it on the news last night. The scavenger community that lives here has been starting the landfill fires, no one is sure why. Day by day the sulphur clouds rising from the dumping ground have thickened. Now they maraud through the skies like battleships, and in the high sectors people complain of afflictions, rhinal, renal, rheumatoid.

One man's trousers are bunched at his knees. A Repeater winds back and swings. The lathi whips through the air again and again. The sound reminds me of Riz's squash racquet, like the rails he'd practise for hours. The Slummer is hopping, clutching his naked arse, yelping miserably. Over the years the East Slum has spread, squat and wet, through the eastern quadrant, a river of blue and black tarpaulin roofs fed by a monsoon of migrants. The landfill scavengers occupy one festering lane of the East Slum, in the shadow of the midden. They've crowded the road with shaky, single-room dwellings.

Sapna lives here. *Leila* lives here. I was nervous even before the Repeaters arrived, all morning my stomach did somersaults. I was trembling as I looked for their hut. Now I feel the blood pounding in my ears, rushing through me, charging every limb.

Slow. Wait for the Repeaters to complete their business. Shift your mind. An old man helps a child squat in an open-air cubicle that dumps directly into the gutter, into a smoking pile the colour of wet coffee grinds. The hand pump, focus on that. Creak-gwoosh-creak-gwoosh, little girls, mothers, hunched biddies crouching around the square concrete basin. Most of the women at the pump are washing utensils and clothes. An old woman occupies a plastic chair. Everyone pretends not to watch the Repeaters. The crowd is arguing, pleading the innocence of friends, children, spouses. A slap rings out, then another. The Repeaters climb into their van, swinging their sticks, slinging abuse. It kicks into life and then down the road, into a self-made swirl of dust.

That moment the wind picks up, bringing tattered ribbons of smoke from the endless fire. Instantly I'm bent double, leaning on my knees, retching and drooling on the road. Acrid fumes scratch at my eyes and throat. When I look up some of the younger children are watching and giggling.

It breaks my heart that Leila has grown up like this. Her delicate, tiny lungs have slowly calcified, these years living in the dirt have lined her face. Now she will be hardly different from these urchins. Sapna, my low surrogate, how could you bring her here, to this forsaken place? Did you really have no choice? Did you teach her, as a child, to go barefoot and barehanded through this diseased dump, scour it for things to sell, for sustenance? I stare down at the streaks of silver saliva I've left on the road, shivering like I have a fever.

A young woman is tapping my spine, the crest of my back. 'Are you okay?' The glare of the sky behind her darkens the face, yet around her there's a shine, a halo. Leila. Grown-up Leila has come to me. Finally we are found. Is it inside that instant, in its hollow denouement, that I understand it isn't her? My thrill is like a speed bump. I wipe my mouth and eyes, nod. The girl offers a sympathetic smile. She starts to walk away. I clutch at her crepe-like sari and cough out a question.

Yes, she knows Sapna Kumar's house. The hut she points to has a washing line spanned across the front, onto which is clipped a single pair of Batman boxers. It's growing again, that tingle in my calves, the sense of an impending moment, of fruition. 'Go,' she says. 'She'll be heading to the landfill soon.'

==

Our home in the East End one evening, Dips visiting. We sat around the dining table, Leila's dolls and blocks scattered across the polished dark wood. Dipanita was zipping up her handbag, preparing to leave, when Sapna skittered up to us, all of twenty, brown eyes shining.

'Get your toys together!' she scolded, mocking. 'What'll Auntie think?'

Faint disapproval on Dipanita's face, a tight smile. 'This girl is too familiar,' she said in English. Sapna was oblivious, helping Leila gather the playthings into a large, sturdy container made from see-through plastic.

'She's fine,' I said. 'They get along very well. She obviously loves her.'

Leila looked up to see if we were talking about her. Sapna tucked the container into the crook of her arm. They collapsed on the carpet in the living room, spilling the toys around them.

Dipanita scraped her chair out and stood. 'You know how to raise your daughter,' she said with a smile. But when we were at the door – I had my back to the room – she clutched my arm. 'Look, look,' she said. 'She's kissing her. Look at that. Nose, cheeks, forehead. How can you allow that?'

'What's the problem?' I asked. 'She washes her bum too.'

'That's different. Not this. There has to be some distance. Propriety. Who knows what's been in her mouth.' She squeezed my forearm tighter, eyes big as a hunting cat. 'They have so many diseases. Stop all this. Promise me.'

'I'll have to think about it,' I said. And I did. What bothered me, I came to realise, was the thought of her saliva on my daughter. I imagined faint, near-invisible lines of spit, slowly soaking into my daughter's skin, becoming part of her. That night I told Sapna she wasn't allowed to kiss my daughter any more.

==

There is no door, it is an oblong hole in the corrugated tin wall, a knotted bed sheet hiding the inside. A flaking blue water drum, half-full, stands sentry. I'm careful not to peek when I knock on the wall. Do not cause offence, be patient. There will be genuine affection between them, love of a kind. But the squalor gives me hope. I can pay, even if I have to promise more than I can manage. My savings from sixteen years at the Ministries, everything I have, all of it can go. Need be I'll go to a moneylender. How much could she ask for, living like this.

A woman responds from inside the hut. Sapna? Or was that . . . was that my daughter? Her smoky, grown-up voice?

At first the change in light is too much, I can't see anything. Slowly a figure emerges from the darkness. The woman seated on the pavement floor peeling ginger root between her legs is dark and muscled. She has close-set eyes, a toothy, slightly manic smile. But this isn't the Sapna who worked for me. The air rushes from my lungs. The dark little room starts to spin. There's no furniture in here to hold on to, I realise, as I crash to the ground.

I haven't fainted, I've landed heavily on my knees. There is no pain. Sapna, this one, she's staring at me, confusion on her gremlin face. 'My daughter has gone to fetch water,' she says. 'You want fridgewater, right?'

'Anything is fine,' I say. The girl enters the hut and with a hint of a curtsy hands over a tumbler, condensation dripping. She's prettier than her mother. She isn't Leila. The water is cold, metallic.

Their home is the size of a bathroom. Spotless – the flatware, the floor, the crisp man's shirt in one corner, everything gleams. In the corner two columns of water pots rise to the ceiling, which is barely higher than my standing height. Three mattresses, tightly coiled, on a shelf near the roof, next to an aluminium chest with a sturdy lock. 'You were asking for me,' the woman declares. She hasn't moved. Her knife shaves the gnarled root with ease. The daughter leans against their metal almirah and slides down to the floor, hugging her knees once she sits.

'My mistake,' I say. 'I was confused. I thought you were someone else.'

A commotion has started up outside again. Through the door I can see people hurrying back in the direction I came from. Sapna swivels her neck. Her daughter jumps up and unfurls the bedsheet at the door, cutting off the light. The mother leans back until she's reclining, resting her head against the far wall. It seems at first she's hiding, but no, she's watching the outside through the long, vertical crack where the tin-sheet walls are supposed to join. In the hut the darkness is gathering weight. What light there is comes from under the curtain, from the walls. Sapna sits up straight. 'The bastards are back,' she says quietly.

'Why are they here?' I ask. Though there is shouting and crying outside we speak in lowered tones.

'They think we're responsible for the fires. We've been trying to explain . . . Ass fuckers, the lot of them.'

Her daughter smiles, showing a stripe of white teeth. Sapna speaks. 'We've been telling Municipal about the fires for so long. Every summer it happens. This year the fire isn't going out, it's out of control. Some parts of the mountain none of us will go near.'

'Why do they think it's you?'

'God knows. They stick their dicks in each other's ears so often it's fucked their brains. Because we work here, I suppose. Because they need someone to blame.' She sucks the moisture from her teeth between sentences. Sffffllllt. 'They've done this before. Once things have died down they'll demand money. Fifteen, twenty thousand, for each person's release. Where will we get that money? I make a hundred a day. Hundred and fifty if I find metal, some unspoilt plastic. Are we crazy? Sffffllllt. The mountain is our livelihood, our only earning. Why would we burn it down?'

'It's been going on for weeks.'

'And what about the stuff coming in from the factories? Drums filled with thick red acid, something like what comes out of a battery. But you can't touch it.' She raises her hand. Skin has bubbled up at the heel of her palm, creating a rubbery pink trench. I feel sick again. 'Sffffllllt. All winter trucks were bringing in those drums. They toss it and disappear. The drums leak all over the place.'

The girl is messaging on her mother's phone, a blue-white light playing across her face. Now she looks up. 'But what are you doing here, didi? Are you from the Slum? Why did you come to see my mother?'

'I'm from the Towers, my dear. Do you know what that is?'

'No.'

'Your mother seems to.' I try to put on an easy smile. 'It's where the Council keeps people who don't fit in. Who broke their rules.'

'What rule did you break?'

'I fell in love.'

Sapna laughs at this, a bitter twist of her lips. 'Remember that,' she tells her daughter. 'Remember this woman.

The Towers is where they put high-borns. Sffffllllt. The people that broke their rules. Sffffllllt. Still they get big, big buildings. Toilet, fans, electricity, flush. Even when they break the rules they're too good to be put out here with us. But us? Our crime is being born. We don't get anything. We don't deserve it.'

Tell her. Tell her I will gladly, instantly swap. Her daughter is in her home, she can reach out at any time, touch her, stroke her hair, teach her how to face this world. I have sixteen years of emptiness. I didn't get to once bandage Leila's knee, help her get over a boy. Leila never kept a secret from me. She never – guilty, laughing – betrayed a friend's confidence to give me a juicy bit of gossip. Stormed out of the room, convinced I'm the biggest bitch in the world. We have been denied the natural arc, the swings between tenderness and dismay, the love between mother and daughter.

But no one must know what I'm trying to do. This is what's important. I must think ahead, to the next meeting, to the Sapna who lives in Officer's Circle.

This Sapna is staring down at the piles of peeled ginger. With the curtain down the air in the hut is thick, close. She looks at me from the tops of her eyes, that sly, gremlin smile returning. 'Lady, you still haven't told us why you're here. Are you hiding from them?' she asks, jerking a thumb at the door.

'No, no,' I quickly say. 'It's just . . . I thought you were another Sapna, one I used to know a long time ago. But you're right, I don't want to be caught up in all that. It's safer in here, if you both don't mind.'

For some time there is silence between us. The abuse and shouting has been replaced by an infant's wail. Sapna nods at her daughter and she ties the curtain to one side again, letting in an angry rhombus of light.

'Do you know there was a fire here also?' Sapna asks. 'Sffflllt. Did you hear about that?' I shake my head. 'The other end of Mahaan Nagar was gutted. Burnt to nothing, all the homes there. Six children died. Hundred families homeless.'

'Did it spread from the landfill?'

'No. The gutter between us is too wide. The fire can't jump it. This was something else.'

'Do you know what caused it?'

'This is what, you people build your fancy things, you don't care what happens to us.'

She's accusing me of things I have nothing to do with. There's nothing for me here, I can walk right out. I take a deep breath. 'What fancy things, Sapna?'

'These things that are coming up all over the city. What do you call it?' She struggles with the English name. 'Sfffflllt. Sk . . . y. Daum. When you build a roof you keep something outside. You put huge air conditioners, pumping cold air into each of the domes. Don't you know what happens behind an air conditioner, what comes out of its ass? That's where the hot air is. Hotter than the sun. They put one of their massive air-conditioning units right next to Mahaan Nagar. Pumping out hot air, all day, all night. One hut caught fire, then another. Soon the whole road was burning. That's how they lost their homes.'

'I'm sorry, Sapna. Can't you do something? Complain?'

'What complain? You think anyone listens? No one cared about the landfill fires for years. Years they've been burning and we've been breathing the air. Our children, our old ones. They only listen when *you* people complain. From inside the walls.'

'I'm not one of them, Sapna. Why don't you understand? I'm not like them.'

'Yes, you are, lady. Whatever they have done to you. That is what *you* don't understand.'

THINGS THAT PULL US TOGETHER

Sapna's letter came a week ago. Since that afternoon an energy is bubbling under my skin that might burst out any moment. I feel faster, more capable. At work they ask why I'm smiling so much. I helped my neighbour clean out the long metal planter she grows her money plants in. I went to the cinema with two women from the fourth floor. Men pawed at us in the crush as we left the hall. I even did my eyebrows, at a small place that I see on the way back from work. The next day I awoke at dawn, just as a dream of Leila ebbed away. In the evening I went to a children's store and bought a colouring book and pencils. At home I coloured in the dwarves, the Dalmatians, the mouse and the duck. When I realised how ridiculous this was I started laughing. My laughter made the apartment sound empty, like a vessel.

In truth, I wasn't sure I would hear back. The second address I found that day in the Records room – it made no sense. Only members of the Council live in the political sector. Somehow Sapna has gone from the Slum to Officer's Circle, the best address in the city, where the Council's most important men have their bungalows. It doesn't seem possible. But Sapna's reply came from there. That's where she's asked me to meet her. This must be where they live.

Once I got over my surprise, I thought about what this must've meant for Leila. Sapna didn't even mention her in the letter. Still I could picture it. Leila has grown up in a big house. With a garden, and trees, clean air, wide roads to cycle on, playmates from good families, an excellent school. Far enough from the margin I occupy that it might be another planet. I should be grateful that Sapna managed to give her all this. Instead I feel deep shame. Fragments of memory suppurate, overcome me. What did I do? I brought sadness to Leila's life. Sapna has been her protector.

The other day, towards evening, it turned cloudy, and for some reason I thought it must be drizzling where they live. I imagined Leila running up the stairs to her mother's room, dragging Sapna from her bed, out into their wet green garden where the trees are like a roof, arms raised to the first rain of the year. The knowledge that I failed my daughter is part of me, I carry it everywhere. Over the years I've covered it over with something hard. But now that I can picture the life Leila has with Sapna, it feels different, like the burning pink skin underneath a blister you've ripped off too early.

They were here all along. Officer's Circle is only minutes from the Ministries. As Leila has grown up, there have been two, maybe three walls between us. When I think about how close we've been to each other all these years, my chest begins to hurt. I have to remind myself that it could easily have been very different. How did Sapna manage to escape the Slum? I have to wonder. All these years I've lived outside the system, outside the sectors, while she has been inside.

Sapna will have kept herself supple and smooth. When I tell Leila our story, won't she study my appearance for signs that I'm her mother? How worn out I will look. I know what the smoke and grime have done to my skin and hair and eyes. And what if Sapna believes, as Dipanita did, that the outside dirt has settled into me, under my skin? That impurity is part of who I am. What if Leila is with her as I walk in, what will her first impression be? It would be a mistake to enter their home on foot. I will take a taxi.

This morning I called a service. The cab that pulled into the badminton court area had a bent, swollen bumper and long silver scratches along the sides almost like racing stripes. Despite this he wanted thousands. Few taxis work the Outroads, fewer still agree to a pick-up in the Towers. I pleaded. He just shrugged, flubbing his lips like a motor revving to indicate it wasn't his problem. Then he was furious I'd made him come out here for nothing, abusing me, my family. This made me feel better. They think it's okay to take advantage because we have so little. When he reached the wall bending towards the main gate, he stopped his car and shouted, 'You sluts deserve to be out here.' Mouth thick with saliva. I just laughed.

On the bus came a terrific surprise. As I bought my ticket, I looked up, and Riz was beaming in the last seat, in his favourite shirt, black with thin navy checks. He glowed like he'd been caught in a shard of sunlight. I went to him almost running.

'You came!' I said.

'Of course. I'd let you do this on your own?'

'I'm so glad that cabbie was an asshole.' I sat down next to him.

'I'd have found you,' he said. I wanted to rest my head on his shoulder. But I knew how it would seem to the others on the bus. Riz looked me up and down. 'New outfit?'

'No, not new. I wanted to look good. I've been trying not to rub my eyes. I don't want Leila to see these circles.'

'Don't worry so much. You look younger. You look happy.'

'I feel happy, Riz. I'm so excited. I even had my

eyebrows done. I haven't felt like this for so long. But it was terrible, this last month. You don't know how worried I've been. And it was my fault. Just like when I tried to phone Dipanita. I'd call and hang up, call and hang up.'

'Why?' Riz asked. We were riding down a broad avenue. The weak morning light made the dust glow pink.

'I was afraid that she'd hear my voice and know instantly what I wanted. Slam down the phone. In a second it would all be over,' I said. 'Leila would never see me, never know about these years I've been trying.'

I suddenly remembered the tribunal, the slobbering, jerking face hanging over my body. I dropped my gaze so I didn't have to look Riz in the eye. He has forgiven you. That's why he's here.

'What did you do?'

'I wrote a letter. That was the mistake. It took her a month to get back to me. Maybe that's why I've been feeling so kicked since she wrote back. Because last month was so horrible. I was hiding at work. I hid in my apartment. I didn't even go downstairs to watch the badminton. Every knock on the door, the sound of the lift, a loud crash, I was sure it was the Repeaters again, come to take me away.'

'But why would Sapna rat you out?' Riz said. 'We were always good to her.'

Sapna's letter is unemotional. I'd written to her in Hindi. The reply came in English. Yes, we could meet. She set a time and date, without recourse to change. This gives me hope. She knows how important this is to me, what I've been through to get her address. She knows why I'm coming. Still she agreed. This means she's been waiting for me too.

I keep rereading the letter for any sign of what will transpire today.

'They must know she's a Slummer,' Riz said. 'Why would they go against their own rules for someone like her?'

'Not just any part. She's in Officer's Circle. The Council's senior men live there. I've been thinking about it a lot. It doesn't make any sense.'

We'd been riding in the shadow of a sector wall. Riz was staring down at the thick, roiling sea of trash on the pavement. The garbage heaved as rodents scurried underneath its surface. Sometimes they burst out into the open, hairy, black-brown things, fat as sin. As we rolled by the neat bricks of the sector wall, I recalled a night from a long time ago.

'Do you remember, Riz, that time one of your girlfriends came to visit from America?'

Riz's eyes went big. He smiled and put his arm around me. 'She wasn't my girlfriend, you nincompoop. We dated for a month in college. She came with her husband! To see our mystical city.'

'I know, I know.' I took his hand. 'I'm not angry now. Do you remember the fight we had, though? Was Leila born then? I can't remember.'

'I think she was. Maybe.'

'I refused to come. You came back late, pretending you weren't drunk. The next morning I blew up, when I found out it was just the two of you, that her husband had fallen sick from something he ate. All night I'd festered at home, wondering what was keeping you there so late. I was sure I knew. I got so angry. I could picture you at the table, leaning into each other, laughing, remembering, stroking hands.'

'Why bring this up now, Shalini? It must be twenty years. Why go over this today?'

I squeezed his hand. 'I don't care about that night. But I remember the fight we had. We screamed at each other so much. I locked myself in the bedroom. I lay in the dark I don't know how long. Only then did I start feeling calmer. Only then could I hear what you'd been saying. That you hadn't intended for it to happen – you were as surprised as anyone when she came down alone – that you were allowed to have a few drinks with another woman without it becoming a storming fight. I could hear you moving about in the hall, in the living room. I wanted to come out and speak to you. Just to say sorry, that it wasn't a big deal. That I loved you. But I couldn't bring myself to do it. It was like my anger had put a wall between us. I felt it looming. The bedroom wall seemed insignificant. But this wall in my mind I couldn't climb over.'

Riz held me closer. He kissed my forehead. 'It doesn't matter, my love. It doesn't matter now. Today we're going to get our daughter. We can finally forget the past.'

'Don't you understand? That's what we are like. I feel it all the time. Everyone tucked behind walls of their own making, stewing in a private shame, like I was that day. They can't come out into the open. Anyone who can afford it hides behind walls. They think they're doing it for security, for purity, but somewhere inside it's shame, shame at their own greed. How they've made the rest of us live. That's why they're always secluding themselves, going higher and higher. They don't want to see what's on the ground. They don't want to see who lives here.'

In the distance, grey, implacable, stood Purity One. From the top of the wall began the Skydome, like a marble roosted on a groove. The dome was opaque in the sun, almost greenish-silver. It glistened like a raindrop.

'I'll feel better when I'm inside,' I said to Riz. 'The dome calms me. They keep the air at such a lovely temperature, like it has just finished raining and the wind is blowing. Purifiers working day and night.' I flashed my identification card as the bus entered a lower gate. Once we were safely inside, I began to take deep lungfuls. 'You won't be able to tell,' I told Riz, giddy, happy, 'the dome makes the air sweet. Empty. Like it used to be before the walls.'

'Think what these filters do to the air outside,' Riz said.

But it's hard to think about that once you're under the dome. The bus lurched through leafy streets, a rainbow sun streaming through in stippled pockets. My stop arrived. I rose to walk down the aisle and Riz was no longer with me. An instant of primal panic. I got off and sat on the bus stop bench and for minutes didn't move. Slowly I aligned my breathing, my every sense, with this hermetic setting. This morning, excitement had knotted my stomach tight as a bowline. I couldn't eat. I packed my sandwich, in case hunger came later. I unwrapped it now. A mynah appeared almost immediately, perching on the backrest at the other end of the bench. The first bite tasted like paper. Still no appetite. I kept looking at my watch. My feet and calves and genitals rang like a temple with a thousand bells, pushing me to get going, burst ahead, race through. I got to my feet. The yellow kohl around

the mynah's eye seemed to glow with accusation. I fed it a
vertex of hard crust and put the rest of the sandwich back
in my bag.

Was Riz right – did we always treat Sapna well? I remember
kindnesses. Giving her old clothes. Three months'
advance, fifteen thousand rupees, when her father killed
himself and it fell to her to make the arrangements.

On that bench under the plastic sky I remembered also
a sweltering noon in our home in the East End, the very
peak of summer. We were in the driveway, the doors
of my car flung open to release the morning heat. The
child seat hadn't been attached properly. I was so angry.
Clenched, bottled fury, at how careless Sapna was being
with my daughter's safety. The sun pounded down,
making blinding lines on the kota driveway. My back and
thighs were clammy with sweat. 'You can't get a simple
thing right?' I shouted. 'How many times!'

Sapna's shoulders had shrunk as she bent her head to the
ground. On her lips a soft, blubbed protest. The guard
stared at us from the gate. I glared back. When I turned
back Sapna was smiling nervously at him. I saw insolence
in that smile, pride, a hollow assertion of status. 'Who
the fuck do you think you are?' I shouted. 'What's so
funny? You're *laughing*? This is my *daughter* you're talking

about. My daughter's safety. What do you think, I'm an asshole? A moron? You'll get away with such carelessness?' As those words came out – my odd, uncustomary Hindi invective – Sapna cracked that smile once again, exchanged another furtive look with the guard. It sent me spiralling to combustion. I took a step towards her with my arm slightly raised. She fell back onto the boot of the car. 'I'll throw you out of here,' I screamed. 'Make sure you don't find another job. You can go back to the gutter you came from.'

A few days later, when things between us had returned to normal, Sapna came to me. 'Didi, I know you get angry. But not in front of the guard, please. Not like that. He thought you were going to hit me. He was telling the servants from the other apartments that if you threatened me like that in the driveway, what must you be doing behind closed doors?'

I wonder if Sapna still remembers that afternoon.

==

The gate is a few minutes' walk from the bus stop. Behind it a narrow lane with a wall on one side with a stubble of dark-green moss. Shade from a long rim of trees gives the lane a mysterious aspect, as if it belongs in a children's story.

I hand Sapna's letter to one of the Repeaters sat on plastic chairs by the gate. He reads with a slow frown.

'This doesn't explain anything,' he says. He's a young, pale man with a moustache turning velvet from mehndi. 'Who you are. Why you're here.'

'I live in the Towers,' I say. 'I came to meet Sapna.'

'Sapna Madam?' He laughs and gestures at his partner, nodding towards me with a mocking grin. 'Look at this one. Sap – *nah* – what a memsahib. What style.' His voice turns gruff. 'Show some respect!'

'Sorry. Sapna Madam. I'm here to meet her.'

'Why?'

'I used to know her a long time ago. She told me to come. Call. Ask her.' I've been holding my breath. When I inhale it's so loud that both Repeaters stare. Sweet-smelling drifts from the mulberry and sonjna trees waft through the crystal air.

The first one looks me up and down slowly. 'That we do for everyone. Not just the trash,' he says, and starts to laugh. On the other side of the gate a rabbit comes out of the undergrowth and puts a pink nose between the bars. Its ears tremble and then it hops away, frightened by the Repeater's boots. The Repeater has marched to the gate. He waits there, phone at his ear, then beckons, ushering me through. I'm about to head on when he calls out. 'Over there,' he points.

Opposing the mossed wall, well spaced from one another, are forbidding metal gates, enormous black, rust, maroon panels dead in the sun. Only the first is wide open, revealing, behind a lick of grass, a small office. Pegged in the grass are three unwashed olive-green tents. This is where the Repeater has directed me. I'm walking through the grass to the office building when a dark face pops out of one of the tents. 'In here,' she says. 'Hurry up.'

The tent flap is horribly damp to the touch. The inside smells of mildew and body powder and sweat. There are a number of cots towards the back, though their bedding looks undisturbed. Three uniformed women sit around a low wooden table, eating fistfuls of shelled peanuts and drinking tea. The fourth, the one who stuck her head out, calls me over. She's round with little arms and an expression of abject disinterest.

'Quick. Don't waste everybody's time,' she says. Her belt, high on the waist, fails to disguise the obscene bulge of fat just under the buckle. The zip of her trousers only makes it three-fourths of the way up.

I'm clueless. 'Hurry up with what?' I say.

'Take it off, take it off,' she answers, tugging the lapel of her shirt. 'Fast. We don't have all day.'

So I'm to strip here, like the servants who enter the high sectors each morning. No problem. I pull the kameez over my head and hand it to the woman. She tosses it to a vacant chair. Another guard stands up now and walks to the front. As I'm unlacing my salwar, this woman upturns my handbag, scattering the contents onto a long folding table. She calls out each object's name and a description, typed by a third uniform into a loud, labouring computer. The guard unwraps my sandwich, examines it, throws it in the trash.

I'm in the middle of the tent in my underwear. I feel fat at my thighs, cold and exposed. 'That also,' the guard says. 'All of it.' Even upright she reaches my chin, not more. I unhook my bra and pad slowly to the chair over which my salwar-kameez is strewn. I drop the bra on the bundle and slide off my panties.

Sapna must've known. She must've known they'd do this to me. The guard takes her security wand between my legs and gently hits the inside of each knee until I stand with my legs apart. A colleague brings a pair of medical gloves. Then her fingers begin working. She starts with my hair, practised fingers streaming through the strands, over the crown, behind my ears. She pats my neck and shoulders and arms. Moves to the torso, dancing her hand beneath each breast in case I've taped something underneath the flesh. She brushes my hips and lightly pinches the folds of skin at my thighs. Now she goes around, so she's behind me. My legs are trembling, knees losing strength. Nothing, this is nothing. Your daughter needs you. The guard squats heavily, with a strained breath, knees popping like corn, she puts either palm on the cheeks of my buttocks and prises the mounds apart. For a second nothing moves. There is no sound. Think only of Leila. The guard's hot breath against the tender skin makes me shiver. Each exhalation seems to enter me, burrowing. Still she searches. She puts her hand to the lips of my vagina, slides rubber fingers inside and deep and once all the way around, a rough forefinger over the tiny, soft ridges. Then she's out. She nods at the other two and walks away. I see her surreptitiously sniffing the gloves before peeling them from her hands.

==

A servant leads me down the driveway. From the first bend you see the mansion, beyond a broad ledge of lawn, a fountain and ice-blue pool and neat rows of potted palms. It looks inspired by the desert palaces: custard yellow, a vast domed cupola straddling the roof, elephants at its four corners with trunks uptwirled, filigreed sandstone balconies. How did Sapna become this? My chest begins to hurt once more.

'How long has Madam lived here?' I ask the boy.
'Many years, didi. Before I started working here.'
'It's very big. Does she have a big family?'

The boy spins around with a puzzled expression. He decides against saying anything. We're standing between a row of low-slung sports cars and one of grey-black luxury sedans. A few feet away begins a dual staircase that sweeps up, like opposing brackets, all the way to a huge oak door. This is where I think we're heading but the servant leads me past the steps without a second glance.

'Where are we going?' I ask. The boy remains quiet. He's figured out I'm not a typical visitor. We walk on a segmented stone path all the way around the manse. A tennis court in the rear is being used as a nursery, with rows of plants in green plastic holders. Crunching through the fading old clay of the court, past sprightly yellow and white gerberas, adeniums, shevanti, some cacti, we come to a matchbox house, the same garish yellow, a two-storey unit previously hidden behind the trees. I can see into the house because the ground floor has a large living room with French windows. And suddenly there's Sapna, unmistakable, though everything about her is so different. She's sitting on a white leather couch with legs folded under her, smiling at something on her phone. She wears a long black batik skirt. Furry bathroom slippers lie carelessly at her feet. She is alone. The boy strides to the window and taps. I put on an eager smile, so she knows that I know she's in charge.

'I was just counting. It's been sixteen years.' That is the first thing Sapna says. She moves back from the French doors with a fixed smile. These past few days, I told myself two things. Don't rush into any demands. Don't be surprised by anything. But Sapna's voice is cultured. Beneath spaghetti straps her shoulders are copper and lightly burnt from a beach holiday. She has acquired the wariness of wealth. She's trying to figure out what I want.

'How well you speak,' I say. I have misread Sapna. What thirst in her to improve, to learn our language, our ways. It's a reminder of how I have lived, like a ship that's been grounded a ways from shore.

'I had a good teacher,' she replies. She returns to her couch and points to a facing chair. The inside of the house gives a strong impression of whiteness – the cool marble floor, much of the furniture, the high walls and ceiling. Jags of orange and bright brown on the modernist paintings only contribute to the effect. I start to feel giddy, like I might vomit. The life I was meant to have. She has taken it all. Sapna is staring at her phone. 'Get us some water, won't you?' she tells the boy without looking up. She turns to me. 'Tea? Coffee?'

I use my dupatta to dab the sweat above my lip. 'Water would be nice,' I say.

'You know, this is the first time we're sitting face-to-face,' Sapna says, with authority. 'Such strict rules you had about the furniture in your house. Sit there, don't sit there.' She gives a short laugh. 'I was allowed to sit on the floor.'

I look down. 'Don't worry,' she says. But there is bitterness in her voice. 'See when Chotu comes back. We also follow the rules. It's tradition, isn't it? No one's fault.'

Chotu enters as if on cue. I quickly drink the water. I've been served in a disposable plastic cup, Sapna in a tapering crystal glass. She affects not to notice. Now it is I who carry the traces of the outside, in my sweat, in my spit. Did she instruct Chotu before? Did he make up his own mind after seeing me? 'You have a beautiful house,' I say. 'It's amazing, actually. How is it . . . how did you convince . . .' She watches with a thin smile, waiting for me to finish. 'How did you come into the political sector? To Officer's Circle?'

'We don't belong here, is that it?'

'That's not what I meant, Sapna. Please.'

'You're right,' she laughs. 'Let's not make this harder than it is. You remember my husband, Ashish?'

'Yes, yes, of course. I didn't know you two got married.'

'That mansion you saw, Mr Joshi lives there. From the Council. Ashish is his Man Friday. When Joshijee became such a big person, he promised Ashish he'd take care of him. He saved my family from the Slum. All of us.'

'You have children?' I ask. My voice is shaking. Breathe.

'One daughter. Lakshmi.' Did her lashes flutter, her eyes lower, just for a second?

'How lovely,' I say, in an even tone. 'How old is Lakshmi?'

'Lakshmi is the one who taught me English. She's very good in studies.'

'I'd love to meet her.' I look around the living room. 'There are no photographs of her anywhere.'

For a few seconds Sapna has a shrewd, narrow look. 'You must be so angry, Shalini,' she says. 'Is it okay if I call you Shalini?'

'Yes, yes, of course. Please do.'

'Thank you,' she says, nodding. 'You must be so angry. All this that has happened. The Council, the Repeaters. These people ruined your life.'

'No, not angry,' I say. 'I understand now that it was inevitable. I learnt at Purity Camp. We invited trouble, the way we lived.'

'You mean to say the Council is right?'

Forgive me, Riz, my handsome darling. You were always too good for me. 'They were right all along,' I say. 'I've thought about it a lot. It took some time to accept, of course.' There is an inch of water remaining in my cup. I drain it before going on. 'At Camp they taught us how to look at things. To understand that everything has an order, a place. When they first sent me to the Towers I couldn't sleep at all. So I would walk at night. Sometimes a pack of dogs would come along with me. They'd walk until a certain distance, then they'd turn back and walk away. I began to realise how much like them we are. They know the limits of their land. They know what will happen if they exceed, it's imprinted somewhere in their brains. The problem is that our brains are more capable, more complex. That's why one part of our brain is forever conceiving things like cars and planes and letters and phones, things that pull us together, while another part of our brain – the safety-first part, the part that keeps us alive – that is trying its best to keep us apart. It's telling us we're too close to one another, the world outside is too complex, too frightening. There are too many people, each one a potential threat. We have to find order in the chaos. We need to break into groups or our brains will freeze from fear. We haven't changed. We still think like animals.'

Sapna scratches her nose. 'I know you think you have to say all this, Shalini. But you can tell me why you're really here.' She stands up and goes to the French windows. Two Repeaters are patrolling the path to the nursery. She taps the windows and they both turn. They march to the porch, snapping to attention a few feet from her, the closed window between them. 'Yes, go on. Tell me why you're really here.'

'It's about that night, Sapna. I have to know what happened.'

'What's the point? Why dredge up these things?'

'I have to know what happened to her. Leila was with you. What did they do to you?'

'I ran. We all did, all the maids. Those men were very scary.' She is still by the French windows, her back to me. The Repeaters are beyond her. I can see their chests expand with each breath. 'Now they're my friends. They do whatever I say.'

'But they found the other children. It was only Leila they didn't find. Where did you hide her? Where did she go?'

'I didn't hide her anywhere. They must've taken her away that night. Put her in one of the schools.'

I jump to my feet. 'Don't say that!' I shout. The Repeaters tense up, staring at me with new curiosity.

'What do you want me to say?' Sapna asks. She taps the window once. The men relax, then saunter away. She walks to the couch and sits down once again.

'You played with her. You were fond of her. You wouldn't leave her like that.'

'I did my job. Nothing more. You were the one who was always worried I was overstepping.'

Deep breath. Do it now. 'How old is your daughter, Sapna? What class?'

'She's just finished her school. Eighteen.'

'But you didn't have a daughter sixteen years ago, Sapna. I know that. You weren't even married.'

'You're remembering wrong.'

'I know what you did. I know how you did it. I want her back.'

'You need to calm down. Sit!'

I realise with a start that I am standing over Sapna, my hands balled into fists. 'I'm so sorry,' I say. 'I don't know what came over me.' I take a few steps back. 'Just one second please. I need to take my medicine.' Sitting down, I pull out one of Iyer's pills from a handkerchief in my handbag, swallowing it with a couple of drops that have clung to my cup, the bitterness swamping my mouth. Sapna stares with her mouth open. For some time we don't say anything. I stretch my legs and lean all the way back in my chair. A soft wave rises from my feet. Sapna is asking me to follow her somewhere. I feel a cold breeze on my face, against my arms. When I come to my senses, we are standing in a tall white gazebo.

Sapna has a slice of white bread in her hands. She tears it into pieces and tosses them into a concrete channel. Huge orange fish break the water's blackness with their grubbing mouths, starting a storm of bubbles. Her shoulders are shaking. Black streaks on her cheeks. I see the tears dribbling down her face.

We aren't alone. Riz is sitting on the wooden railing of the gazebo, directly behind Sapna's back. He makes me so angry I begin to shout. 'How could you, Riz? All of this is your fault. You did this. Had to be a tough man in front of your fucking friends, fight everyone. You couldn't keep your mouth shut. Now I have to face all this alone. Sixteen years alone.'

'Don't give up, Shal. You're almost there,' Riz says softly. He climbs down from the railing and comes to me. 'You'll see her before you know it. I promise.'

'Liar! Don't say things you can't guarantee. You were supposed to keep us safe. Your daughter. Me. You couldn't even stay alive.'

'Stop it, Shalini!' Sapna says, though not loudly. I turn to her. 'Do you know you've been muttering things to that pillar for five minutes?' Sapna asks. She squeezes one hand in the other, her face anguished. The tears flow slower now. 'What did they do to you, these people? They've taken your mind.'

The gazebo is bounded on three sides by a tall hedge. Repeaters stand in separate clumps beyond the hedge. I can't think of what to say.

'Turned you into a junkie,' she goes on. 'God knows you had your problems, but you didn't deserve this.'

'These pills are nothing. I can stop them anytime.'

'They've given you the wrong idea, Shalini. You're very confused. About times, dates. About your daughter. Lakshmi has nothing to do with you. She's my own daughter. You didn't know about her because you never cared to ask.'

'That's not true,' I say. My head goes side to side very fast, an involuntary gesture. 'It's just not true. I know you have her.'

'Will you be quiet?' she hisses. 'You really don't

understand what you're doing.' She looks around once again, staring intently through the leaves of the hedge surrounding us for any sign of movement. A group of Repeaters chats less than twenty yards away.

'I'm very sorry, Sapna. I lost my cool inside. But don't deny me this. Please. For her sake.'

'Just stop, Shalini. Stop all this right now. Do you realise what happens if anyone hears? They will launch an investigation. We're in the heart of everything here. The centre of power, of the city. The top of the pyramid. There can be no question of impurity. Even the hint of a suggestion that my daughter is a girl like Leila and my husband won't be able to do a thing. They would take her away immediately. I'd never see her again.'

'Sixteen years I've looked for her. Please don't do this.'

'You've looked for someone else! You've gone crazy! Why can't you understand? Leave my daughter and me out of it. You'll get us both into trouble.'

'Can I talk to her? Just a few words.'

'She's about to leave for her tennis class. What are you going to say? She's my daughter. What could you possibly say that would do her or you any good?'

I fall at her feet. In old movies, when the once-arrogant hero does this to the penurious girl's father, reconciliation begins. 'Please,' I sob. 'Please.'

'You're making a scene. You have to leave.'

I touch my forehead to her feet, weeping still.

'You're only making this worse.' Sapna kicks out her right foot, firm enough that I have to raise my head. 'Stand up. Everyone is looking. They're going to wonder who you are. If my husband finds out I let you come here I'll be in huge trouble. Stand up. Stand up at once.'

She barks out an order. Two Repeaters march to the steps of the gazebo. One puts his fingers softly on my elbow, like he's carrying something dirty. 'Will you reconsider?' I say, soft as I can manage. 'Sapna, please.' She has turned her back. The Repeaters lead me down the gazebo steps and into the garden. We reach the nursery. Now the plants all droop. As we cross the green-lattice shelter, I wrench my elbow free and spin around. The gazebo is empty. Sapna has gone inside. All I can see, tucked behind trees, is her two-storey house.

For some seconds I stare. The world absolutely still, no leaf or limb astir. Suddenly the silver glint of a window pulling open. On the first floor, framed in the perfect square, there is a girl. Her mess of black curls lifting lightly in the wind. She is perhaps a hundred yards away, but I can see she's wearing a white, collared shirt, a tennis shirt. The Repeaters have hold of me again, one on each arm. I'm struggling, snapping, trying to bite. They won't let go. They're dragging me away. The girl doesn't seem to hear or see. At just that moment the sun comes out from behind clouds and the distance between us falls to nothing. Like a dawning light her face becomes visible. Her nose is broad at the bridge. Eyes like dark emeralds. She has large, square incisors and skin the shade of butternut. She's beautiful. Her smile crinkles her face at the cheeks, bracketing the almond tips of her lips with two majestic arrowheads. Double dimples, dimples unlike any other, dimples like my mother and I have. What's that she does now? She no longer looks out the window. Is she practising a tennis stroke? Is that a wave? She is swinging one brown arm, a white sleeve riding up her shoulder. She keeps making that gesture. She is calling me.

ACKNOWLEDGEMENTS

MJ Akbar, Zarine D'Monte, Louisa Joyner, Imogen Pelham, Dharini Bhaskar, Mukulika Akbar, Shonan Purie Trehan, Raoul Bajaj. Each gave generously of their time and talent when I needed it most. I will never forget their kindness.

My mother Mallika was my first reader, sending patient, thoughtful critiques of chapters that it must've been clear would soon be discarded. Her empathy and insight have always guided my work. She pushed me to go further into Shalini's plight, to hunt for beauty in her sadness. This story is far richer because of her.

It was my great fortune to work with Shruti Debi, an extraordinary editor and first-rate agent. In precise, devastating emails she would indicate where I had gone wrong. At each stage she seemed to understand my intention better than I knew how to express. She was vital to turning this effort around.

Shanta Rana Akbar walked with me each step of this road. She read everything, took every setback and fillip with characteristic calm. She has filled my life with a happiness I could not have imagined.